# TINY TWISTS

Stories That Zig When They Should Zag

JEFF W. LINZEY

EverBetter Books

*Tiny Twists*



*Tiny Twists* is a work of fiction. All incidents, dialogue, and characters are products of the author's imagination, and are not to be construed as real. Any resemblance to real persons is entirely coincidental.

The graphic on the title page and the start of each chapter is from Pixabay.com and is used by permission. The Cover image is partially created using Microsoft Copilot.

ISBN:979-8-9960827-0-4

EverBetter Books

# DEDICATION

For my beloved wife Nicole,
whose steady love and unwavering support
have carried me through every season of life.

And to Jocelyn, Adelaide, Michaela, and Eleanor.
Thank you for filling our home with laughter,
chaos, and the stories that inspire my own.

# CONTENTS

# CONTENTS

# INTRODUCTION

A preface should not dawdle. It should open like a door at dawn—quick, clear, inviting—and let the stories inside speak in their own voices. So here is the distilled truth of how these pieces came into being.

I was raised in a home where imagination was not a luxury but a living current. When answers ran thin or certainty slipped away, Dad offered a simple, liberating command: "Make it up." Over time it became a family shorthand, then a mantra, then an echo that could be heard from room to room—MIU, the three-letter spark that turned hesitation into invention.

My brothers absorbed the phrase with the same reverence and mischief that I did. We challenged one another, nudged one another, sometimes collided creatively, always pushing the boundaries of what a story—or a moment—could become. Those early rhythms stayed with us. They still do.

Years later, when I sat before a list of writing prompts, MIU rose again like a familiar melody. Each prompt became a doorway I stepped through with shifting strides—sometimes bold, sometimes wandering, sometimes circling back to see what shimmered in the corners. I experimented. I played. I let the page surprise me.

The result is this collection: varied in shape,

restless in spirit, stitched together not by genre or structure but by the impulse that birthed them. Some pieces are light and quick. Others linger. Some tilt toward humor, others toward tenderness, others toward the strange and delightful. What unites them is the quiet inheritance behind them—the father who encouraged invention, the brothers who sharpened it, the childhood that made creativity feel like breath.

If these stories feel diverse, that is by design. If they feel like someone enjoying the act of creation, that is true. And if they feel like echoes of a life shaped by encouragement, competition, and a steady invitation to imagine—well, that is exactly what they are.

Jeff Linzey

# 1

# LUCY

Lucy was 12 years old when she finally learned what real love looks like. Born to teenage parents, Alexis and Joshua, who often reminded her she was an accident, Lucy grew up knowing she wasn't wanted. Like over half the babies born in New Mexico, her parents weren't married, but for a little while, it seemed like something was keeping them together.

When she was 8, she realized her dad was selling drugs. Her mom gripped her shoulders, fear sharp in her voice, "Don't ever tell anyone. If you do, they'll come take Joshua away, and they'll hate and despise us. Promise me you'll never tell a soul!"

Her breath hitched, tears blurring everything as she choked out, "I won't. I won't. I promise!"

When she was 10, Joshua got picked up near her school for possession with intent to distribute and sent to prison for three years. After shouting things she couldn't take back and collapsing into a shaking heap on the floor, Alexis rose without a word, went into her room, and slammed the door. That evening, Lucy poured herself a bowl of cereal, the clink of the spoon echoing in the quiet house. She brushed her teeth and changed her clothes with the same somber silence before crawling into her bed, feeling quite alone. In the morning, Alexis was gone.

She went to school and told her teacher about it, who told the principal, who called child services. Whispers rippled through the classroom. Lucy's stomach dropped, and her already fragile ego was shattered when her situation was made public in front of her class and child services took her into custody. "Taken into custody" may not be the preferred phrase for people to use, but that's what it felt like to her.

Forms, questions, waiting rooms—everything felt endless through a bureaucratic maze she'd never imagined. It didn't seem like the same level of detail applied to would-be foster parents. What was likely only a couple of days in reality felt like an eternity before she was placed into short-term foster care. Seven other kids lived there, with an unspoken hierarchy she learned quickly, all away from the unobservant eyes of Rick and Debby.

The next two years saw her moved to three different homes with feeble excuses or justification if any. Nevertheless, here she was, a 12-year-old mistake that nobody wanted, nobody cared about, and no real chance of happiness.

That's when she arrived at Daniel and Karen's home. One child of their own that was about grown and out of the house, and two infant foster kids—actual brother and sister. The older kid was essentially non-existent in her life, and while Dan was out working, Karen largely had her hands full with the little 'uns.

Karen seemed to know what was going on in the house and always had a watchful eye, even though she was very hands off. A few days into her stay, Lucy walked from the pantry with a box of cereal. She stood in the kitchen, unsure where anything was, until Karen quietly pointed out the silverware while setting a bowl on the counter. After the first month, Lucy relaxed a little, but didn't want to get too comfortable. It was only a matter of time before she'd be forced to move again.

Once Lucy seemed to let down her guard, Karen started trying to be a lot more involved. No yelling, no belittling, and apparently genuine interest in Lucy. It was weird. Lucy didn't quite know what to do with it. But then again, she didn't know much about life. Everything was uncertain, everything was unfair.

She didn't try to be a problem, but trouble

seemed to follow her, and she regularly found herself sent to the office or threatened with detention. Nor did she try to pick fights with Dan and Karen. It just sort of happened. She knew it was only a matter of time until they pushed her out and she would have to go to another home.

But Dan and Karen gently and firmly applied more rules and guidelines, more restrictions, and got more involved in her life. What was with them?

Then the night came that Dan and Karen asked her to come have a seat in the living room. "This is it. This is where they tell me I can't live here anymore and that they don't want me." Lucy was sure of it.

[Karen] "Lucy. We both want to talk with you. We know life hasn't been fair. It hasn't been easy. And you've had to deal with things that no kid should ever have to deal with. It's hard. It'd be hard for anyone."

[Lucy] "Yeah, yeah. Just skip to the part where you kick me out and send me off to some other home."

[Dan] "What? No, no... nothing like that. We want to let you know that no matter how hard you push us away, we're not giving up on you. We're here for you, and we wish you would share with us what's going on. What's it like in your new school? Who are you friends?"

Lucy rolled her eyes, failing to suppress her doubt of Dan's sincerity, all the while wanting it to be true. The tense "family meeting" itself would be enough to drive most young girls to tear up, and Lucy was no different in that regard. The dissonance between her expectations and what Dan and Karen were saying added confusion that also showed through her moist eyes. "You say that now." She swallowed hard—her throat felt thick.

[Karen] "We'll say it tomorrow too." After a brief pause, Karen continued, "It seemed like you were finally starting to relax a little, and then you started acting out."

[Lucy] "Maybe I don't want to stay here. After all, you've been getting meaner and meaner and not letting me do much of anything anymore."

[Dan] "Lucy. Real love sets boundaries. Real love is unconditional. It's because we care about you that Karen and I have started cracking down and setting stricter rules.

Lucy scoffed and let loose another eye roll, this time avoiding eye contact afterward while trying to process what was actually being said.

[Dan] We're trying to be fair with the consequences and match them to your behaviors and tendencies. We want you to thrive, but people only grow and develop the right way when there is structure and guidance. That's why we've added all the additional systems.

[Lucy] "You don't love me. Nobody could love me. I was an accident… a mistake! How could anyone ever love a bastard like me?"

[Karen] "Did you know that one of the most famous stories in the world starts with an unplanned pregnancy and a couple that wasn't yet married?"

[Lucy] *Sniffling* "Really?"

[Dan] "It sure does. Has anyone ever told you the story about Mary and Joseph, and their baby named Jesus?"

[Lucy] "You mean, like that church stuff? I've heard something about it, but it's just that sissy stuff to make people scared to do bad things."

[Karen] "Some might talk poorly about it, and as for it being a gentle and forgiving religion, you're right. But it's not about doing good things because you fear hell; it's about loving God so much you want to do good things. The Bible even talks about strength and power and all the ways that God helps us. But it all starts with his love for us. The story of Jesus' time on Earth isn't all sunshine and roses, and despite Him trying to teach everyone to love each other and take care of each other, many people hated Him. They didn't want to let go of their hate and treat others well.

[Dan] "But he loved all of them—even those that hated Him or tried to hurt Him. God loves US unconditionally, and sets rules for us to follow because of that love. He sets the perfect example of what real love looks like. Can we tell you the story?"

[Lucy] "I'm not really sure. I mean . . . I don't know."

Karen didn't move closer, but she angled her body slightly toward Lucy, leaving space—an invitation, not a demand. Lucy noticed, not even pretending she didn't.

After a long moment, Lucy scooted an inch closer on the couch. Not touching—just... nearer. Testing. Waiting to see if Karen would flinch or shift away.

Karen didn't.

[Lucy][Barely above a whisper] "I don't... I don't know how to do this."

[Karen] "You don't have to know. I'm here."

Lucy nodded once, tiny and stiff. She let her shoulder tilt a little toward Karen—not leaning, not cuddling, just letting gravity pull her a fraction closer. Karen didn't move, didn't comment, didn't make it weird.

Lucy exhaled shakily. "Can I... just sit here? Like this?"

Karen smiled softly. "Of course."

Lucy didn't look up, but she let herself stay there—close enough to feel the warmth of someone who wasn't leaving.

Not trust. Not yet. But a beginning.

# 2

# THE WIDOW

"Can I please just have ooooooone more?" Harper pleaded.

Looking out the apartment window as the rain clouds smothered what light remained in the already gray city, Alyssa replied, her annoyance unmistakable, "You said that last time.... And the time before."

"Pleeeeeeeeeeese? I won't ask for anything else ever again."

The number of times the little girl had broken that promise matched the number of times she'd made it. Still, Alyssa caved, squeezing her eyes tightly shut and wishing away the migraine that no amount of coffee or cigarettes could cure.

A familiar refrain echoed in her mind—Jackson never would have been so soft or feeble as to give in to a four-year-old. Why did it have to be like this?

3

# THE DEADLIEST HIGHWAY IN AMERICA

Out the side window, the sunset had turned the sky into complimenting hues of reds, purples, and blues. The meadow was only occasionally obscured by the odd passing car. Looking out the side, there was nothing to suggest anything other than perfection as Jacob was on his way to take Ashley out to dinner and propose.

Out the front windshield, against the blinding backdrop of the setting sun, was a sea of red lights as far as one could see. Not an unfamiliar sight in Florida, but not one that Jacob was expecting on this particular Saturday late afternoon.

Jacob grimaced and cocked his head, muttering under his breath, "Why are they such stupid drivers. Maybe don't speed so much and you wouldn't hit the car in front of you. Maybe just pay attention to the road and not your...." His phone buzzed. Though on silent, he could still hear it, and he reached over to pick it up. It was a Google Maps alert about higher-than-normal traffic, and a potential accident up ahead.

"Really!? You think I don't know? This is stupid."

The vehicles in front of him inched forward, but not because traffic was moving... they simply kept creeping closer to the cars ahead, each driver likely frustrated and eager to move on.

Jacob was desperate to get to Exit 33 (SR 33 / CR 582) to Lakeland, where his girlfriend Ashley lived. She was a student at Southeastern University and though a year behind him, was set to graduate Magna Cum Laude at the end of the winter semester. She was smart, beautiful, and for some odd reason, quite smitten with Jacob.

He had just passed the exits for Epcot and Animal Kingdom before grinding to a halt, and the detour sign said to take exit 55 for US-27... just under ten miles away. Nevertheless, this was going to take some time.

"WHYYYYYY!" Banging on the steering wheel, Jacob could feel himself losing it. It wasn't just any date, this was *THE* date, and he had left Orlando with plenty of time to make it and still be able to stop for a Dr. Pepper at the corner gas station to calm his nerves. He had planned everything to a T, talked with Mr. Martinez and gotten his blessing, and designed the most romantic and perfect of dates—odd to some, but sure to be special and in line with all of her quirks and preferences.

Jacob had red-shirted his first year at University of Florida (UF), hoping to get a chance at the big time. Despite his size, strength, and skill, he ended up riding the bench behind someone bigger, stronger, faster, and better in just about every way. Leading into his "senior year," he sustained a knee injury that required surgery and put him on the injured reserve. His football career and hopes of playing the NFL were dashed. Not that he expected too much. He earned his bachelors degree and planned to work in Orlando for a year before enrolling in the following year's MBA program at UF. Not ideal, but he knew better than to put stock in a pro career. That was merely the dream. At least... the dream before he met Ashely.

He could have taken the starting position at a number of other Division I schools, but coming from Central Florida, UF spoke to him in a special way. And like every faithful red-blooded American in Central Florida, he despised every other college... those with Division I football teams, anyway. Southeastern University was fine. In fact, it wasn't much on his radar until Ashley.

*HONK!!* The vehicle behind him laid on their horn, and he stopped reminiscing long enough to see the three-car gap ahead of him—shocked that the cars behind him didn't simply swoop around and fill it.

"Man... if I had my say, I would really lay into whoever caused this jam!" Jacob looked down at the clock, then confirmed the time on his watch, then—hoping both other time pieces were mistaken—picked up his phone and checked the lock screen to be sure.

Just a couple more miles to the turnoff, and the detour would only add about fifteen minutes to the normal travel time. What the heck was going on?

Another bevy of emergency vehicles approached from the rear, tentatively making their way through the lanes on the other side of the barrier. "Wow.... Something pretty serious must have happened. Normally they just eke their way through the same direction of traffic and force everyone to squeeze to the sides. I wonder what it is?"

As Jacob approached his detour, he was starting to take the exit as he looked ahead. Despite squinting to account for the remaining half hour of daylight gleaming over the horizon, he was certain he recognized the overturned car, and his heart dropped.

He turned-off in the partial shoulder of the exit and threw the vehicle into park, jumping out and nearly getting hit by another frustrated detour-taker. He ran toward the site of the accident, only to be stopped by a deputy and an imaginary barrier created with flimsy caution tape.

"Officer, you don't understand!"

"Deputy."

"Excuse me? What?

"You said 'Officer,' but I'm a Deputy Sheriff. Call me 'Deputy.'"

"I'll call you 'Deputy Dan' if you want, but I think that's my girlfriend's car up there. I need to go see if she's OK!"

"I'm sorry, son. You'll have to wait until we've cleared the scene. I can't tell you anything more at this time."

"Can you at least tell me if she's OK? Can you at least tell me if it's her!? Her name is Ashley. Ashley Martinez. Please!"

"Look here, mister, you know about as much as I do. But I was told to keep everyone a significant distance away until the coroner gets here and they can remove the bodies."

"Bodies!"

"Calm down, calm down. You're getting all worked up for nothing. It's probably somebody else. I-4 has the highest number of deaths per mile, so they say. This kind of thing happens every day."

"Please!"

"Turn around and go back to your vehicle. We could ticket you for stopping in the exit. You're lucky we're busy dealing with other matters at the moment."

In exasperation and at wit's end, Jacob turned around and trudged back to his truck. Not even stopping to make eye contact with the steady flow of drivers exiting along the detour, Jacob walked in obvious melancholy.

Distraught about what even to do, he turned the keys in the ignition and sat there. Their designated rendezvous now half an hour in the past.

Another five minutes passed as he sat there. Does he turn around and return to his apartment in Orlando? Does he go see her parents to let them know?

He mindlessly put the truck in gear and followed the GPS to the pre-entered coordinates for her dorm.

As he approached the final turn, he saw a bar up ahead. Clicking "exit" on the navigation, he tossed his phone to the passenger seat and drove past her street toward the bar.

He unloaded on the bartender, relaying every detail of the day and making sure to explain why tonight was so important. Oh, how everything changed in the blink of an eye . . .. An hour-long detour of a blink.

Jacob put his face into his hands and sobbed.

While still early for a Saturday night, the usual crowd began to trickle in, and the barkeep encouraged him to leave or at least move to the corner.

Jacob paid his tab and went back to his truck.

Still unsure what to do, he fumbled around the empty Dr. Pepper bottles and loose papers in the passenger seat, paused with his hand on the ring box, then moved it aside and picked up his phone.

Three missed calls from Ashley, one voicemail, and two texts—some of which came while he was talking to the deputy, and most of which came while he was drowning his sorrows.

"Jacob! You stupid jerk. I thought you were going to pick me up for a nice date. Why did you stand me up? You have a lot of explaining to do. There better be some darn good reason you're not here!"

The first text message read: "Just saw something about an accident on I-4. Are you OK? Should I be worried?"

The second message read: "Just called the hospital and they said it was some long-haired guy that drives a white Corolla kinda like mine. He's not OK. But neither are you! Call me."

# 4

# THE BOARD MEETING

[Chairman] <u>HELL-o,</u> everyone, the time is 3:30 p.m. Underworld Mean Time on February 3rd of the year 2026 CE—I'd like to call this meeting to order.

[Mammon](Under their breath) He's always doing that… making insipid puns about Hell.

[Chairman] We have a quorum with representation from all nine circles, including additional guests. Providing us a word of the day is Agares. Please give him a <u>WARM</u> welcome.

[Agares] Let's dip our toes into the woeful yet expanding Gen A terminology. It was a toss-up which one you'd like the most, so you get both:

Dog Water: Something or someone that is "dog water" is extremely bad or low quality… like the dregs from bowls of the hellhounds Cerberus or Garmr.

Drop common loot: this is an accusation for someone that is basic and insignificant. Great for use when tormenting those of the current generation, especially those into gaming and even more especially for those that like to do dungeon crawling.

[Chairman] Thank you Agares. Please take a look at the folders in front of you; they contain the minutes from the last meeting. Any objections or corrections?

[Unintelligible murmurs as the demons review the previous minutes.]

[Chairman] The minutes are hereby approved. With that I'd like to move to the main order of business—a review of our target audience and key strategies. Despite an increase in total souls across the last three consecutive quarters, there are some interesting trends and recent developments that I would like to highlight for the group as we tee up some proposed refinements in our tactics. Take a moment to review the charts and info graphics before you, and I will proceed.

During the last session, I led our reviews of Customer Segmentation and Behavior—what type of people fit into what categories, and how their actions are predictable— emphasizing psychographics and habits of those selling us their souls (i.e. why they do what they do and how they do it). This session, we will deep dive Industry Trends and Drivers, otherwise known as what they're doing and why they do it. Breaking technologies like Artificial Intelligence are providing an open canvas, with users placing blind faith into the veracity and authenticity of its results. We are working with several industry leaders, integrating our content into their models to establish a baseline within their responses. We are already seeing high degrees of addiction and social isolation, with the majority of AI prompts and interactions already revolving around companionship. People are foregoing real-life relationships in real life for the echo chambers of social media and AI interaction. We will reinforce these initial gains with progressive discourses that lead to sales.

We will soon have multiple major search engines supporting our cause and suggesting with predictive text that the most common phrases following every major question word has to do with selling their souls. For example:

Who . . . can sell their soul?

What . . . can I get for selling my soul?

Where . . . can I sell my soul?

When . . . do I have to sell my soul to get the best deal?

Why . . . should I make a deal to sell my soul?

How . . . much can I get for selling my soul?

Not only are developing technologies supportive of our business model, the social and economic factors influencing the market are also trending in our favor, and consumer values are approaching record lows.

A quick review of Porter's Five Forces... don't forget that we have but one competitor, and He hasn't changed His strategy since the dawn of time. Nevertheless, it's worth remembering that He has a strong draw over most people. While there is no threat of new entrants to compete for people's souls, we can use regular refreshers on our bargaining power and that of those contemplating the value of their souls. Understand what our future tormentor is offering to the mortals. We should find more-immediate and more-tangible substitutions we can dangle in front of humanity. Let's continue to up our game.

A noteworthy development is occurring across the dog water that is humanity [the Chairman looks at Agares and gives subtle nod of recognition and approval], it's worth noting that normally, struggles and trying times turn individuals to the Son of the Most High God, but current circumstances are such that even though everyone is struggling, they're turning on each other instead of turning to prayer. To paraphrase Yoda and Palpatine in one fell swoop, everyone is scared, angry, hateful, and generally suffering because some with power who are angry are attacking the defenseless... they are using their weapons and striking down the targeted groups with all of their hatred. The bitterness and depression is glorious! Ha ha ha. This is suffering that leads to more suffering, and I think we have a golden opportunity to harvest more souls. And here's how we're going to do it.

We will maintain our traditional methods with 60% manning, shifting 20% to focus on emergent technologies with Belphegor taking point on the AI efforts, and the remaining 20% will support Dagon's initiative to develop Phishing emails + Clickbait.

As an aside, Dagon has some promising feedback from some of the prototype phishing emails and clickbait. He has devised compelling prompts, and even distilled a binding sale of one's soul into as few as three clicks of the mouse. Really promising stuff here. We might even be able to work some of those methodologies into some of the complicit AI organizations so that within a few prompts is a link into Dagon's binding agreement protocols.

Before closing, I would like to provide a cautionary tale. You would do well to avoid the cavalier and poorly researched market approach that Iblis recently undertook. Iblis, stop licking your wounds for a moment and share your story.

[Iblis] Satah-tariqu fi al-jaheem (Burn in Hell).

[Group Response] Nahnu fee Jahannam (We are in Hell).

[Iblis] As you all know, people's search histories are a great source of insight for their temptations, proclivities, and vulnerabilities. While following up a few other leads, I decided to do a snap campaign on everyone that searched for or viewed "Getting it

Twisted," then proceeded to waste the next few quarters fruitlessly targeting people curious about short stories, AND NOT what I thought were the vile lowlifes (prone to dropping common loot) and prone to finding themselves with Minos in the 2nd circle. As the Chairman said, make sure you do your research thoroughly before you end up on a cold streak and failing to collect souls for over a year.

[Chairman] This brings us to the end of the agenda items for today. We will forego the open mic today.

[Lilith] But I have a few points I would like to bring to order.

[Pazazu] Shut up Lilith. You always have points you want to bring up, but having to listen to you go through them all is torture.

[Chairman] Pazazu—your observations is well-received. We will go ahead with the public comment session. Lilith—please step up to the podium.

# 5

# THE MOST SIGNIFICANT YEAR

"I lost count of how many times I've fallen off the wagon," Betty lamented to herself. "There's something comforting about a box of wine after a long, trying day… and something troubling about using an entire box to cope with just about anything—well, anything except a family reunion or game night. But I digress. I do love boxed wine."

The problem wasn't the drinking itself, nor even knowing when to stop. She never went to work drunk or hungover, but most nights had blurred together for nearly three years, and she needed it to end. Betty and James were two years married when they conceived, two and a half when she miscarried, and three when he filed for divorce.

"It feels like a lifetime ago—and also like yesterday. I remember the newlywed butterflies, the joy of saying 'We're pregnant,' 'We're having a baby,' all the 'we's.' And I remember the blame that followed—the 'You lost the baby,' all the 'you's.' So many memories packed into such a short time."

Their first anniversary was a delight; they'd never really left the newlywed phase. Their second anniversary was joyful and hopeful. Even without a positive test, they were trying. Shortly after the second anniversary, Betty peed on a stick, and both their hearts lit up with glee.

Now, two and a half years divorced, Betty had a different kind of milestone to celebrate. Losing the baby was the worst. James's betrayal was unexpected and cruel, though he'd never truly been the dependable-for-life kind of man. Perhaps it was better she learned the truth early—but the timing was unbearably unfair. It took a year and a half to hit rock bottom. Only then could she face her life and begin clawing her way back.

For the longest while she blamed herself. Lord knows that James blamed her. But after losing control for so long, it felt like an act of God that kept her from going over the edge and finally brought her back to her senses. "Thank you, God, for helping me to see things clearly."

She had been sober for 363 days. Tomorrow would be huge!

She told her girlfriends only two weeks before the event; she'd tried to get sober three times before and always fallen off the wagon. This time was different, and the only difference was God.

She'd stumbled into a midweek service at the church down the road. They were hosting small groups and had a ladies' group that was meeting that night. Had it been any other night, or any other church, or perhaps the Mormon ward across the street, who knows where her life would be right now had it not been for that moment.

Tomorrow would mark 364 days—one day shy of a full year since she chose to stop drowning the grief of losing her baby, her marriage, and nearly herself. The miscarriage had hollowed her out, and James's blame had carved the hollow even deeper. For a long time, she believed she deserved the emptiness. For a long time, she believed she had caused it.

But tomorrow, she would stand among women who had held her story without flinching. Women who didn't blame her. Women who didn't leave. Women who reminded her that healing rarely happens alone.

Her sobriety wasn't just a milestone; it was a resurrection of the self she thought had died the day the pregnancy test turned negative and the marriage papers turned final. And maybe that was the miracle—God meeting her in the lowest place and walking her back into the light, one trembling step at a time.

She didn't know what the next year would hold—joy, sorrow, something in between—but she knew she would meet it sober, awake, and wholly herself. She knew she would carry the memory of her baby with tenderness instead of shame. She knew she could think of James without collapsing.

Maybe that was enough.

And for anyone listening, anyone aching, anyone whispering into the dark:

*You are not alone. Someone will hear you. Someone will stay. Someone will help you rise again.*

# 6

# J WILLIAM RICHARDS III ESQ

J. William Richardson III, Esq., left his home in rural Louisiana at the age of fourteen, determined never to look back. Nothing his family did quite qualified as abuse, but if the constant negativity, partial neglect, and persistent sense of unwelcome—how they tore him down whenever he achieved even the smallest success—helped him make up his mind. If he didn't get out from under them, they would keep him down forever.

"Camo," as his childhood friends used to call him, had a lifelong tendency to keep his head down, in large part due to the metaphorical bucket of crabs he used to live in. His fondness for avoiding the lime light did not stop him from graduating with honors, first from Northeast High School, then Louisiana State University, and finally LSU-Baton Rouge School of Law. His concentration in corporate tax law suited his sharp mind for numbers and his obsessive-compulsive need to cross Ts, dot Is, and balance the books.

It might not come as much of a shock, despite the awful pun, that Camo Richardson (camouflage riches) accumulated stealth wealth—something in the ballpark of $27 million across sundry investment vehicles. From what Horatio Alger might call "unrespectable circumstances", the respectful young man made good on the American Dream, and a mere few years after graduating law school, through hard work and smart investing, was far from his upbringing, but could never get past his insecurities and need to escape it.

With his affluence, and while maintaining a low profile, Camo travelled the world, volunteering with various Non-Governmental Organizations and self-funding a few missions and outreach trips. That's where his rags to riches story stops cold. On the return flight from a trip to provide aid in the Central African Republic, his plane was lost at sea somewhere off the western coast of Africa.

Missing and presumed dead, a new cast of characters enter the scene.

**Dr. Denis Mukwege Foundation** joined by the **World Food Programme**: Charitable Non-

Governmental Organizations (NGO) operating in the Central African Republic (CAR).

**Maddison**: The high school girlfriend that claims Camo fathered her child before he left for college.

**Jed Michaels**: The flat-fee attorney hired by Camo's siblings.

**Isabella**: The fiancé.

Each party showed up with assorted claims, all questionable, and all with the support of the law... but which law would hold out.

The NGOs claim that Camo created a will during his month-long aid visit prior to his demise, leaving all of his estate to support the causes after death that he most vigorously supported during life.

The state of Louisiana recognizes "Forced Heirship," where dependents under the age of 24 (or disabled) automatically inherit a portion of the estate regardless of any will or previously expressed interests of the deceased. Maddison claims that Camo is the biological father of her 7.5 year old twins and she is entitled to half of the estate — 25% for each child (up to two) in accordance with state law.

Jed Michaels holds out that there is no will, the dearly departed had no children (legitimate or otherwise), and that the current-est girlfriend is trumping up their relationship in a ploy to secure the estate of the decedent.

Isabella, by far the most likable of the characters, lived in Baton Rouge. She was a special needs teacher in one of the local elementaries, but she and Camo went to the same church, and grew a fond respect for each other on a missions trip to Cameroon two summers ago. They officially began dating last year and Camo proposed to her last Christmas. They spent the summer in Colorado, renting a condo in the Springs near where Isabella's family lives. According to Isabella, they held themselves out as married and Camo intended to move his practice to Colorado. While Louisiana does not recognize common law marriage as occurring in-state, it does recognize common law marriages from other states. Colorado has the least restrictive relevant laws, and holding themselves out as married, cohabitating, let alone their pious background and unlikeliness to live together outside of marriage are all more than enough for Colorado to recognize the marriage.

Trial was set, the parties' lawyers notified, and everything in place for what promised to be the most exciting family case of the year. Things had already gotten nasty in the lead-up to getting a slot on the docket.

That's when the message came in:

*International freight ship THE MERIDIEN TRADER reports finding a man stranded on a desert isle. Man claims to be J. William Richardson III., of Louisiana.*

Isabella seemed to be the only one excited about the headlines.

# 7

# ESCOVITCH SNAPPER

It was their 4th anniversary, and he and Rachelle were walking along the beach. A cool breeze lifted her hair, and joy rang through her laughter. Her smile stretched wide as the sun warmed her skin and shimmered through her flowing hair.

* * *

Jeremy was safe and well attended. They did everything they could to ensure his comfort—regular meals, clean sheets, even fresh flowers arranged by the window.

* * *

Rachelle ordered the lobster bisque, and Jeremy had the escovitch snapper, and they shared a bottle of Albariño. The restaurant sat just a short walk from the cottage they were renting, and the day begged them to stroll.

* * *

Jeremy's room was at the end of a long hall, and everything was tidy and purposeful. Large windows were plentiful, and even the long halls had natural light pouring in as they went out in all directions from the main lobby. The dining and recreation halls were exceptional.

* * *

Back in the room, Jeremy ran his fingers through her hair as she unbuttoned his shirt—the slowest part, since her wrap and swimsuit slipped free with a single pull. She flung his trunks toward the suitcases, and they tumbled into the sheets.

* * *

"Jeremy. Jeremy!" No amount of calling or volume could pull him from the memory. "Mr.

Evans, It's time for your sponge bath. We're going to begin now."

* * *

It was a beautiful day, a casual afternoon, and such a delightful anniversary getaway. The decision to skip Sandals and its crowds was genius—seeming better with each day they spent on the Island. How could anything top this? Rachelle didn't bother dressing as she wandered to the bathroom to wash up.

* * *

"Good evening, Mr. Evans. I'm going to wheel you over to the rec room. Some of the other guests that will be glad to see you."

"Don't bother Jessie... all he ever does is mumble something about Rachel and snapper."

"No man, it's 'Rachelle.' She was his wife. After the cancer took her last year, he never snapped out of it.

"More like, 'Snappered out of it.'"

The joke hung in the air, but Jessie ignored the tasteless pun. He rested his hand on Jeremy's shoulder and wheeled him toward the rec room, where sunlight pooled across the floor. Behind Jeremy's distant gaze, Rachell's hair still fluttered in the island breeze.

# 8

# PIERCING EYES

The mirror never lied.

All of her bad decisions stared right back at her.

There were the obvious ones like consistently bad dietary choice, and only less obvious like the baggy eyes from all night bingers and poor sleep.

But there were also the non-obvious ones—the ones deep inside from the depression and self-loathing that moved inside her and drove her to some dark thoughts about self-harm.

She usually wore a subtle smile and avoided eye contact. Put up a strong front and cheerfully returned greetings and "how are yous."

But the mirror never lied.

# 9

# APATHY AND ELEVATORS

Walter always did well in school, especially math, but had no particular ambitions to steer him in any particular direction. During his senior year at Reading Sr High School in Pennsylvania, he participated in a trip to NYC. What caught his attention wasn't the plethora of monuments and skyscrapers; rather, it was what was inside most of those large buildings. For reasons he couldn't explain, he found himself fascinated by the elevators. Thinking nothing of it at the time, they finished their two-day excursion in the city, and started heading back to Reading, PA.

The bus ride back was perhaps the biggest indicator of the general ambition and expectation among his peer group. Somehow, the conversation steered toward the subject of what people were going to do after graduating.

"I'm already working at Home Depot. There are opportunities to promote or move to different positions. They even said if I want to transfer to a different store, that's an option."

"I'm going to do the Nurse Tech program and work in the hospital"

"I work at Walmart. My mom needs a lot of help around the house with my younger siblings, so I'll just keep doing that and help out as much as I can"

"I'm enrolling into Reading Area Community College. Hopefully I can get into Alvernia University after that"

"I got a job as Boscov's. They said if I get my diploma and am willing to work the busy hours, I might be able to move from being a stocker to working on the floor."

"My dad's a manager at a Penske. I'm going to work for him."

When attention fell on Walter and it was his turn to chime in about his post-high school ambitions, his eyes darted to each of his peers. Even though their ambitions were low, at least they had something in mind.

"I don't know. I haven't really thought about it much."

In fact, Walter hadn't thought about it at all. He could always figure it out later. In the meantime, there were daily achievements to unlock on some of his favorite mobile games. When he got tired of whittling away his time with those, he leaned his head against the bus window and watched as they passed fields, pastures, houses, and all manner of routine things that had no potential bearing on his future. Thinks didn't look great.

At a mandatory session with the guidance counselor going into his final month before graduating, Walter was pressed to answer the question of what he was going to do. She wasn't going to let him go until she got an answer.

"Walter—if you could do anything in the world… within reason… what would it be?

"Well…," his voice petered out, his gaze fell lazily around the room, as if an answer or at least some motivation was somewhere lying around that he might find. "I kind of like elevators."

"Elevators? That's your plan? Elevators?"

"I guess. I mean… is that thing? Can I, like, do… elevators?

"Hang on, let me see." Punching away with her thumbs on her smart phone, the counselor's posture froze with her eyes fixed on her little screen. "Well I'll be…. It would appear that there's a low barrier to entry to work as an elevator technician. It's pretty dangerous, kind of like being a lineman, but not really much more dangerous than working at a steel mill."

And like that, Walter found himself well on his way to a 6-figure, dead-end job in the city. Plenty of physical demands, not a lot of social interaction required, and a starting salary of $90k—almost triple what everyone else on the earlier bus trip was looking at.

And so, after graduation, Walter found a small place in the city, and worked.

That amount of money for a young kid in the city is a great way to get in trouble. But with as little motivation and as few interests as Walter had, he spent most nights at karaoke bars or going to shows in town.

His apathy and loneliness were quickly turning into depression, and he knew what he was doing wasn't sustainable. But what else was there? "Nothing Really Matters!"

That thought kept running through his mind. Even at work, while rewiring the elevators or working on the hydraulics that prevent cars of people from plummeting 30 floors to a crushing death, or entire buildings from going up in flames… "Nothing really matters." He knew this was becoming precarious. But what?

The show he attended that weekend featured "Queen Nation," the premier Queen tribute band in the world. It was a high-energy escape from the monotony of his dead-end, repetitive, and dangerous-yet-non-exhilarating job. The jolt of enthusiasm he felt at the show was different. He used that energy the following night at Karaoke and even enlisted the support of some of his regular rivals to join him for a rendition of Bohemian Rhapsody. They crushed it! And the whole bar's uproarious standing ovation sealed the deal. Walter finally felt excited about something… motivated even. For the first time in as long as he could remember, he had a dream. Taking to the internet that night, he Googled "How to Join a Queen Tribute Band."

The application process was grueling. The competition for limited positions fierce. The auditions looming. Just getting a manager of a legit Queen tribute was difficult, and the few friends in his life challenged why he would jeopardize or throw away his steady, high-income job for such a weird dream. He left those nay-sayers behind.

The most exciting lead was for a group out of Australia. Well-reputed across the globe, and performing all over (at least all over Australia)… that could be fun.

Didn't pan out.

There were a few other opportunities, but the only response—if he even got one—was rejection (sometimes in harsher words than others).

Walter didn't fancy himself as the greatest Freddie Mercury of all time, but he was finally motivated about something, and ready to work for it. He watched all the footage. Took piano lessons. Practiced replicating the specific sounds, vocal harmonies, and mannerisms of rock's greatest frontman.

A rare opportunity arose with "Bohemian Queen," not only one of the premier tribute bands, but particularly renowned for their 100% live performances of Bohemian Rhapsody. Walter took it as a sign. From that night during Karaoke when he stoked his fire and passion in life, he was a man on a mission, and this was the divine confirmation he was doing what he was meant to do.

The audition was nothing short of doing Bohemian Rhapsody from start to finish with Bohemian Queen themselves!!!

The lights, the stage… the only audience was the manager sitting near the front and the bandmates on stage. This was the moment on which his entire future hung.

Walter could feel himself channel the spirit of Freddie Mercury into his performance. He was on fire, and nailing every note. His use of the mic stand, his actions on the keys as he tickled the ivories. He was doing it.

". . . Nothing really matters . . . to me."

The manager, whose chilled introduction and stone-cold demeanor did little to instill confidence, now had a subtle smile across his face.

# 10

# THE BIRTHDAY WISH

Fewer than twenty-four hours ago, Mattie had been telling his dad what he wanted to do for his birthday. The request was big, but nothing ever felt too big for Chief Technology Officer Matthew Sr. The fact that Mom disapproved only made it more appealing—not just for Mattie, but especially for Matt Sr.

Mom and Dad had divorced four years ago, which meant double birthday presents, double

Christmas presents, and a father who tried to compensate for his absence during the few visits Mattie got each year. This year promised to be the biggest birthday. Matt Sr. had made a name for himself as a CTO, but he'd earned his first million doing web design for one of Silicon Valley's biggest firms, including a long partnership with Extreme Adventure Experiences, Inc.

"I love everything about extreme adventures, and I want to do all the things you did, Dad. Can we do like… three or four of them tomorrow?"

"Well… I have a meeting with the board at ten, but after that I should be free. What did you have in mind?

A giant smile crept across Mattie's face, his eyes widening with excitement.

* * *

Now it was 2:00 pm on his birthday, and he had not seen this coming. His heart pounded, his mind raced. "He… he just jumped out of the airplane without a chute!"

Matt Sr. knew a lot about computers and a lot about extreme adventures, but not much about managing his time—or keeping a promise. Perhaps that was why everything happened the way it did. There's no question that was why Elizabeth had left him. He didn't overindulge in alcohol, and he would never have considered cheating on her—at least not in the traditional sense. He was too committed to the job, to the company, and to the prestige of being the highest-paid CTO in the Valley to realize that he was cheating her and Mattie out of what they wanted most.

* * *

So there Mattie was, sitting all alone in his dad's mansion, watching Point Break for the first time and reeling at the moment Johnny Utah jumped out of the plane WITHOUT A CHUTE!!!

Not long afterward, Mattie wandered back to his dad's small shelf of movies beside the giant flatscreen. Let's see... if Dad has every streaming service known to man but still kept this tiny collection of movies, there had be a reason. An that last one was AWESOME! Just like Mattie imagined skydiving would be.

Right next to Point Break was Cliffhanger.

"Hmmm.... Never heard of it. Let's see...." He thumbed through a few more movie titles. "The Rock"? Couldn't hurt to try it.

Mattie knew how to use a credit card, so ordering pizza was easy. Plus Mom wasn't there to say no. Another dinner at Dad's house all by himself. Mattie sighed in disappointment. "Dad's not going to keep his promise. I hate myself for always believing him!"

The Mercedes pulled into the long driveway a little after seven. "Mattie," Matt Sr. called. "I'm home, son. I'm sorry for missing your birthday. I promise I'll make it up to you. How long are you here before you have to fly back?"

## 11

## THE TRANSCRIPTIONIST

Have you ever noticed the people lingering at the periphery of major international business transactions or diplomatic conventions. Rows of booths line the walls, filled with a slurry of headphone-clad professionals. Those are translators, and they typically earn between $50,000 and $100,000 a year. Many are paid by the word. Some hold specialized qualifications—legal, medical, or fluency in multiple languages. But the most lucrative skills are often discretion—and a willingness to bend one's morals. Daniel White possessed all those skills and more.

By day, Daniel freelanced for top translation agencies, filling their most critical gaps and high-impact assignments. Whether the task involved complex multinational negotiations or obscure linguistic niches, Daniel was the unsung force keeping global transactions alive. He spoke thirteen languages fluently and could absorb the basics of a new one in as little as a week when needed. His grasp of legal, medical, architectural, and military terminology was so precise that many assumed he was an expert in each. Perhaps he was.

His day job was respectable enough—legitimate, steady, and dull. But Daniel's mind refused idleness. Without a complex system to unravel or a linguistic puzzle to devour, he grew restless. So at night, he sought sharper edges and higher stakes—as a transcriptionist.

Trusted for his discretion and quietly renowned among the world's most notorious organizations, his deft fingers and agile mind flew a mile a minute, turning raw audio into immaculate text in any typeface—or language—requested. It began two years earlier, when DMG Mori in Germany urgently needed translation support for a detailed contract involving cutting-machine tools and CNC-controlled lathes and milling systems. Daniel got the call.

Little did he know a prominent Yakuza emissary happened to be visiting the Japanese CEO—and witnessed Daniel in action. Daniel was professional, unflinching, and so precise in tone that he could imply threat or disdain with the slightest inflection. When the job was done, he bowed with cool formality, shook hands, and left. The Yakuza reached out discreetly soon after. Word spread quickly. Soon the Sinaloa Cartel, the Russian Bratva, and even the Hells Angels sought his services. Bound to no one, but usually accepting the offers, he only refused work with the Triads.

Transcriptionists listen to recorded audio and convert it into a text format. They use shorthand notes when listening to the recording, expand these for future use and edit their transcriptions prior to filing them.

Leaders across these organizations trusted Daniel with the most intimate details of their lives and operations. He captured every nuance, in any language, without flinching or betraying even a flicker of doubt—no matter how gruesome the content.

The true irony is that the US Intelligence and Law Enforcement Services enlisted Daniel's services, too. Terrorist threats, financial trails, decrypted banking chatter—whenever the FBI, CIA, NSA, or Homeland Security faced their toughest linguistic puzzles, they turned to Daniel. While it would be a conflict of interest for some, so divorced of emotion was he, spurred on by super-power-like OCD, that no one on the government side even had a hint that he was supporting the other side, too.

No one ever knew the real Daniel White—only his prodigious output from his nightly endeavors.

And that's how it remained until the day he died.

The unsung hero of international business and politics, the trusted guide through volatile multilingual negotiations, and the quiet key to dismantling some of the world's most dangerous criminals. So much of the interconnected world depended on Daniel. They never knew the breadth of his connections—and he never told.

## 12

## CLOSE THE DOOR ON YOUR WAY OUT

Though he would never admit it, opera spoke to Eric and touched his soul in a way words could never express. He wasn't embarrassed about it, but as a matter of self-preservation, he kept his inner drama enthusiast under wraps.

"I guess I'm a closet thespian," Eric mused, tickled with his own droll humor. He was straight, no doubt about it, but loved a good play on words. And he loved to sing.

Eric lived two hours northeast of Atlanta in Stephens County, and just last year, the principal disbanded the school's performing arts clubs and cancelled the drama department. The local sets of 59 Brim Bloods and Rollin 60s Crips, though hell-bent on killing each other, regularly jumped in new recruits by targeting performers. The more flamboyant or theatrical the student, the bigger the target. A few years earlier, one of Eric's older brother's classmates had been killed in just such an initiation. Those gangs were the worst part of living in Toccoa and made life there almost unbearable.

Just one more year to go, and he could graduate and get out of there, finally free to be himself. His bold, boisterous, bass-baritone self. He just couldn't at this juncture in time.

His grades were good. Not great, but solid. And he did just enough math and science to get by. But he loaded up on music and languages, working ahead until he'd taken all the French and Italian the school offered, eventually requesting special permission to study German remotely through a school on the other side of Atlanta. After finishing the assigned homework, most nights he'd pick his way through Bizet and Berlioz, Verdi, Wagner, and Wolfgang Amadeus Mozart. The French and Italian operas were breezy reading, their scores leaping off the pages and straight into his heart. German was still difficult, but knowing much of the music already made the words easier to tackle.

Early in the spring, as basketball season wound down, there was a gang-related shooting in the parking lot after one of the games. Eric didn't know the victims, but the incident reminded him to keep his passion on the down-low and sharpened his urgency to finalize his escape plan. UGA's Hugh Hodgson School of Music offered a performance-based scholarship he was determined to earn. It was only a matter of practice.

He began staying after his eighth-period music class to work on his audition. Weeks away from graduation, while practicing in his happy place, the door opened and two thugs walked in.

"Yo. Who you, and wha' dya doin'?"

Eric froze.

He'd been so excited to practice that he didn't notice his classmates hadn't closed the door all the way, and his music was spilling out into the hall.

Before him were five arias meant to showcase his bass-baritone fach. But nothing from Gounod, Rossini, or Mozart in front of him was going to get him out of this predicament. And nothing about his taste in music would ease the tension of this moment.

Orff's "O Fortuna" was on blast in the internal soundtrack of his mind.

Sors immanis
Et inanis
Rota tu volubilis
Status malus
Vana salus
Semper dissolubilis

But it wasn't just in his mind. Eric was so stressed, he was belting out the Latin lyrics with more passion, volume, and intensity than any of the pieces he had been practicing only moments earlier.

"Dude! Dude! That's that song from the movies! Like… 6 Underground. I just watched it two nights ago." The first thug smacked his friend's shoulder, excited by the music and recognizing it from a movie he'd seen on Netflix less than forty-eight hours ago.

Eric's heart pounded so hard, he could hear his own pulse. The muffled sound of the two muttering as they walked out was cut short when the door finally clicked shut, sealing off all sound.

Music nearly got him killed that day—but it also saved his life. When the door finally clicked shut behind the two boys, Eric stood there trembling, breath shallow, heart still pounding in his ears like timpani. The room felt smaller, the air thinner, as if the danger had squeezed the space around him.

But then he looked at the door. Closed. Sealed. Silent.

A door left open had almost ended everything. A door closing had given him another chance.

He let out a shaky laugh. Music had betrayed him, exposed him, nearly delivered him straight into the hands of people who would never understand him. But music had also been the only language powerful enough to disarm them. It was ridiculous. It was terrifying. It was perfect.

He gathered his sheet music with steadier hands. One day, he promised himself, he'd walk through a different door—one he chose, one that opened into a world where his voice wasn't a liability but a gift.

For now, he locked the practice room behind him.

And for the first time, he understood that the right doors don't just open. Sometimes they close to show you where you're meant to go next.

# 13

# EAGERLY AWAITED RETURN

Departing from home was always torture.

A month seemed like such a long time. But for his young children, it was a significantly larger percentage of their lives.

His wife missed him before he left and took that loneliness out on him the day or two preceding any trip.

The first week was always brutal.

Time seemed to accelerate proportionately to his business.

The last week flew by, but the last night was full of anticipation and scarce an opportunity to sleep.

Alarm set for 2 a.m., he couldn't relax his mind enough to nod off, eager to get back to his family and his dog.

## 14

## QUITTERS NEVER PROSPER

*This wasn't the first time the young couple had quarreled over the matter. Picking up in the middle of a tense engagement, the intensity has escalated higher than normal, and instead of shutting down and retreating into herself, she digs in sticks to her guns.*

[F] "You said you were gonna quit!"

[M] "And I DID quit! But a lotta good that did me! Not like you were any help in the matter anyway!"

[F] "All I been try'na do it is take care of you. You gon' go get yo'self killed and leave this family high and dry!"

[M] "All I do, I do for this family! There's no break to be had, and it ain't easy out there."

[M] *Hanging his head in desperation*

[F] *Approaching matter-of-factly with a stern look*

[M] *Looking up to make eye contact without really raising his head*

[F] *Pausing mid-step and starting to reach out, before continuing to him and putting her arms around his neck*

[F] "We appreciate you. We really do. We just love you too much to see you go. ... You said you'd quit."

[M] "I will. I really will."

# 15

# WHAT'S MY QUESTION

| . . . | . . . | . . .

The blinking line "insertion point" in his Word document seemed to taunt him.

"What is your question? What are you going to type? You don't know, do you? You don't have any f*!@#$% idea."

It would be maddening if it weren't accurate in its torment; instead, it was simply demoralizing... depressing.

Enrique was a straight-A student throughout high school and finished his bachelor's with a 3.98 GPA. His master's work was more tailored to literature than education, but he was breezing through it and already had his sights higher.

The Gonzalez family was bright, and after seven generations in Chesco, just south of Philly, it was hardly accurate to call them immigrants anymore. Still, the brown skin and trace of an accent never stopped others from exuding prejudice onto them.

Enrique's great-great-grandfather had been the first in his family to attend college. His great-grandfather earned an MD and served at the Children's Hospital of Philadelphia. Two of his aunts became attorneys, and his father has always encouraged him to pursue an MBA and join him in business. Instead, Enrique pursued and MA Lit/MSEd combo wondered whether he might teach someday. Maybe at a university? Maybe after he proved himself—did something that made him feel qualified and acceptable.

It was the "maybe" part that trapped him.

"I know I love academia. I love learning. love sharing that love to help others learn. And higher ed is practically in my blood. If I spend a few more years of school, I'll be better qualified for professor positions, I'll get to learn more, and maybe I'll figure out what I really want."

Talking himself into the resolve to pursue a PhD was the easy part. Now he had to choose a specific question—one worth answering—and build a research proposal around it. Choosing and deciding from among options had never been a strong suit. Enrique even avoided Starbucks because their menu overwhelmed him, preferring instead the simple certainty of a Nespresso variety pack at home.

It was now September, and he would finish his master's program in the spring. PhD applications—proposals included—were due in a couple of months. It was already September.

Every few days, after mustering the motivation to open the blank document, the blinking cursor stabbed at his thoughts like a large-gauge needle through the eye. At least he'd named the document, so he could reopen whenever he worked up the courage. It's title: "Draft Research Proposal – Enrique Gonzalez."

He still had nothing.

| . . . | . . . | . . .

"What's my question?"

He leaned back, rubbing his eyes, letting the silence settle. All his life, he'd waited to feel qualified before stepping forward. But maybe the question wasn't something he found. Maybe it was something he grew into.

He placed his hands on the keyboard. The cursor blinked. He blinked back.

"Fine," he whispered. "Let's figure this out together."

And for the first time, the blank page felt less like a threat and more like an invitation.

# 16

# A LITTLE KINDNESS AND COMPASSION

A dozen scarlet roses greeted her as Bridget walked in the door. The bouquet was an opulent curation of long-stemmed, high-perfection roses in a hand-tied arrangement with baby's breath and other greens. Each rose carefully selected and symmetrical and the colors so vibrant, the contrast to her subtle pastel décor was stark. It was easily $600-worth of flowers sitting on her Ikea table in her small but comfortable apartment.

The card in the flowers read: "I will never forget the day we met, nor how I've fallen more and more in love with you every day since. You enthrall me.

The fragrance of your perfume lingers in my mind, and the way you walk leaves me distracted thinking about you. Thank you for being in my life. ~Terry"

The knock on the door startled her as she was reading the note. Sliding the dime-size cover off the peep hole, Bridget placed one hand lightly on the door and leaned into to identify the visitor. It was a middle-aged, stocky man, with a neatly trimmed beard and she could smell the muddled mix of Pine-sol, tobacco, and WD-40 just looking at him. Tony was the apartment Super. A kindly and responsive man that was quick to make repairs and kept the whole place running like clockwork—even if he was always smoking on the roof when not in the service areas of the building.

Bridget opened the door and offered a polite but colder-than-normal greeting. Tony hesitated for a moment, perhaps taken aback by the lack of warm small talk like he usually shared with most of the residents. Shrugging it off, he continued. Glancing over Bridget's shoulder and into the apartment at the extravagant flower display on the table, he made eye contact with Bridget.

"Sorry to bother. Just wanted to make sure you got the flowers. They were delivered to the building, but I didn't want to just leave them down by the mailboxes in the common area. I went ahead to put them in the room for you. They came in the vase and look trimmed. The water's a bit cloudy, so I assume it already has the plant food stuff in it that often comes with flowers. Anyway, what's the special occasion? Not to be nosey, but I don't recall seeing anyone around, and that looks like a nice anniversary bouquet."

Bridget looked back over her shoulder at the flowers, but didn't say anything.

"I'm Sorry. I suppose it's none of my business. You have a great day, miss. Let me know if you need anything." Tony left, cheerfully greeting the residents four doors down that were coming out as he passed them in the hall.

Bridget walked over to the window and looked out the blinds. A moment later she closed them and walked back over to the table with the flowers. Ever since showing a bit of kindness and compassion to help that smarmy IT guy pick up the tools and miscellany that he dropped when the office bully tripped him, Terry wouldn't leave her alone. He'd done something to remote into her computer and arrange all her desktop icons into a heart. The calendar on her office wall seemed askew and was turned to the wrong month. And he'd friend-requested her on Facebook. He was quickly demonstrating all four signs of a stalker: fixated, obsessive, unwanted, and repeated.

And now the flowers . . . . He knew her address.

# 17

# THE THREE LITTLE WASICU AND THE BIG BAD CHAGA

Once upon a time, in a land far, far up north, an evil despot ruled his land of cloudy water with an iron fist. His lands were bountiful and produced a cornucopia of food and plants, but he did not like to share. Not only did he want to keep everything for the people of his own land, he wanted to get rid of all Wasicu people not born in his lands.

Their motherlands hadn't had much for them, so three little Wasicu went into the world to find their fortunes and moved to the land of cloudy waters. Despite working many decades to build homes and establish their families, not all were as prepared as others for the "Chaga," the brutal predators the tyrant used to do his bidding. One of the Wasicu had a home made of straw, one of them a home made of sticks, and the third had a brick house.

The Chaga approached the straw house and banged on the door.

"Little Wasicu, Little Wasicu, Let me come In. Your kind are not wanted and you cannot win."

The first little Wasicu, caught unawares, nevertheless replied, "Not by the hair on my chinny, chin, chin. We help, not hurt your land. Your argument's a straw man."

The Chaga snorted, chuffed, and retorted, "Then I'll huff, and I'll puff, and I'll blow your house down." The house came tumbling down, but those inside hopped out the windows as it was falling. They jumped into their cars to drive away, but the Chaga got them anyway.

Puffed and proud, the Chaga continued along to the next house.

"Little Wasicu, Little Wasicu, Let me come in. We're bigger and badder, you're smaller and sadder"

The second Wasicu had heard the commotion from before, but left without many options, defiantly declared, "Not by the hair on my chinny, chin, chin!"

"Then I'll huff, and I'll puff, and I'll blow your house down!"

As the stick house toppled, the kindly old Wasicu fell down. A good Samaritan nearby came to her aid, but the merciless Chaga would not be stayed. It grabbed it and beat it and killed the Samaritan there where it laid.

As amped up as ever, spurred on by their ruler, the Chaga kept on getting crueler and crueler. Approaching the third house, the one made of brick, they reveled in downing the straw house and stick house.

"Little Wasicu, Little Wasicu, Let me come in!"

"Not by the hair of my chinny, chin, chin."

"Then I'll huff, and I'll puff, and I'll blow your house down."

The Chaga, try as it might, could not get the brick house to budge an inch. The Chaga was frustrated, nay 'twas enraged. Looking for another way in, it climbed atop the house and started to go down the chimney. The clever Wasicu lit a big fire place atop it a giant pot of water. The Chaga lost its grip and fell into the pot.

The Wasicu, not particularly sure how to season a Chaga soup, ultimately added some beans and a few spices he had on hand. What a dinner he had.

# 18

# COLORS OF THE UNSEEN

Professor Emeritus Lionel Thatch—distinguished astrophysicist, honorary wizard (self-appointed), and proud owner of a cardigan older than most of his graduate students—had a habit of making pronouncements that sounded like prophecies.

"Possible," he would say, tapping his chalk against the board, "is merely the polite cousin of *inevitable*." For Professor Thatch, little excited him like the journey from "impossible," to "possible," to "proven."

His students loved him for it. The university's administration tolerated him. And the scientific community, by and large, had learned that when Lionel declared something "impossible," it was time to start writing grant proposals.

So, when he announced, at the annual Symposium of Practical and Impractical Physics, that he had finally completed his "Perceptual Recalibration Engine," the audience leaned forward. When he added that it allowed humans to *see* wavelengths of light normally invisible to the eye, they leaned back again.

"Impossible," muttered Dr. Hargrove, who was distinguished, elderly, and—according to Clarke's First Law—very probably wrong.

Lionel only smiled. "Seeing," he said, "is believing."

The device itself was disappointingly mundane: a pair of glasses that looked like they'd been assembled from a welding visor, a colander, and a handful of Christmas lights. It hummed faintly, as though embarrassed by its own existence.

"Behold!" Lionel declared, placing the contraption on the head of his long-suffering graduate assistant, Mina.

Mina braced herself. She had once tested Lionel's "gravity-resistant loafers" and spent the afternoon drifting gently across campus like a lost balloon.

The glasses flickered. The lights blinked. The colander vibrated.

Then Mina gasped.

"Professor . . . the air is full of . . . colors."

"Of course it is," Lionel said. "Infrared, ultraviolet, terahertz emissions, cosmic background radiation—why should the universe limit itself to the narrow band we call visible light? That's like judging a symphony by listening through a kazoo."

The audience murmured. A few skeptics squinted at Mina, as if trying to see what she saw through sheer force of will.

"Describe it," Lionel urged.

"It's like… like the world is layered," Mina said. "There are garlands of heat rising from everyone's skin. The ceiling is glowing with microwave scatter. And Dr. Hargrove—"

"What about me?" Hargrove asked suspiciously.

"You're . . . iridescent. Like a soap bubble made of equations."

Lionel beamed. "Elegant, isn't it?"

The murmuring grew louder. A few scientists began edging closer, curiosity overpowering their stoic sense of dignity.

"Let me try!" exclaimed Dr. Patel.

"Me next!" jostled Dr. Nguyen.

"Absolutely not!!!" bellowed Dr. Hargrove, who then immediately added diffidently, "Fine, but only for a moment."

One by one, they donned the glasses. One by one, their skepticism dissolved into wonder.

"It's like magic," whispered Patel.

"Not magic," Lionel corrected gently. "Just technology sufficiently advanced."

Clarke's Third Law hung in the air like a satisfied ghost.

Soon the room was buzzing with delighted pandemonium. Researchers dashed about, waving their arms through invisible currents. A pair of engineers attempted to high-five a passing neutrino. Someone tried to hug a microwave hotspot. Hargrove, to his credit, admitted that perhaps he had been "premature" in his assessment of impossibility.

Lionel watched it all with the serene pride of a gardener admiring a particularly unruly patch of flowers.

Mina tugged his sleeve. "Professor... what made you think this was possible in the first place?"

Lionel chuckled. "My dear, the only way to discover the limits of the possible is to wander a little way past them into the impossible."

Clarke's Second Law, delivered with the casual ease of a man quoting his grocery list.

"But really," he added, lowering his voice conspiratorially, "I just wanted to know what the universe looks like when it isn't pretending to be ordinary."

Mina smiled. "And now everyone else can see it, too."

"Exactly. Seeing is believing. And once they believe, well . . . the impossible doesn't stand a chance."

The symposium ended with three broken chairs, one cauterized curtain, and a waiting list of two hundred scientists eager to borrow the glasses.

Lionel considered it a resounding success.

After all, he thought as he packed up the humming, blinking, colander-topped device, the universe had always been magical. It was only polite to give people the chance to notice.

And somewhere, in the swirling, radiant tapestry of wavelengths only he and Mina could see, the cosmos winked back.

# 19

# SEEDS OF DISSENT

In the year 2242, humanity finally achieved a utopia of perfect efficiency. Every aspect of life was optimized, streamlined, and stripped of unnecessary frivolity. And nowhere was this more apparent than at mealtime. Food, once a source of pleasure and culture, was now a mere matter of functional nutrient delivery. The daily ration for every citizen of the gleaming Global Collective was a flavorless, beige paste called "Nutri-Slurry," dispensed from chrome spigots in every home. It contained all the necessary vitamins, minerals, and macronutrients to sustain a productive life. It was clean. It was logical. And for those that knew what food could be, it was unbearably, soul-crushingly bland.

But in the forgotten corners and shadowed alleys of the pristine metropolis, a rebellion was simmering. A revolution against the literally tasteless society. They called themselves "the Foodies" and were a small, clandestine group of individuals who risked everything for the simple pleasure of a good meal.

Their leader was a man named Jean-Luc, a descendant of a long line of French chefs. His face, usually creased with worry, would light up with an almost holy fervor when he spoke of the "Before Times," a mythical era when food was not just fuel, but an art form. His second-in-command was a woman named Paloma, a fiery Latina whose ancestors had been masters of spice and seasoning. Together, they led a motley crew of flavor-worshippers who scrounged for ancient cookbooks, cultivated illegal herb gardens on hidden rooftops and secret rooms with specialized lights, and bartered for contraband ingredients on the black market.

One evening, while the Foodies gathered in their secret hideout beneath a decommissioned nutrient processing plant, the air was thick with the forbidden aromas of garlic, onion, and roasting meat. It was a stark contrast to the sterile, ozonic atmosphere of the city above. Tonight was a special occasion. Jean-Luc had managed to procure a whole chicken, a creature so rare it was spoken of in hushed, reverent tones.

"Mes amis!" Jean-Luc proclaimed triumphantly, his voice trembling with emotion as he held up the plump, pale bird. "Tomorrow will linger in the nostrils and tastebuds of generations to come. We may not all return to gather again. But tonight, we feast!"

A respectful silence fell over the group as Jean-Luc began to prepare the chicken with the precision of surgeon. He rubbed it with a mixture of salt, pepper, and a precious pinch of dried rosemary from Paloma's rooftop garden. He stuffed its cavity with a lemon, a small, wrinkled orb that had cost them a week's worth of energy credits.

As the bird roasted in a makeshift oven fashioned from an old incinerator unit, the Foodies prepared the side dishes. There were potatoes, smuggled from a rogue agricultural zone, roasted with garlic and thyme. There were carrots, glazed with a precious spoonful of honey. And there was wine: a dark, rich liquid fermented from stolen grapes. The Efficiency Enforcers had classified the beverage as a Schedule-A controlled substance, illegal in the highest order.

The meal was a symphony of flavors, a riot of sensations that stood in defiant opposition to the bland monotony of their daily lives. The chicken was juicy and succulent, its skin crispy and golden. The potatoes were fluffy and garlicky, the carrots sweet and tender. The wine was bold and complex, a warm caress on the palate. And for the first time in a long time, the Foodies felt truly alive.

But their celebration was short-lived. A sudden, loud banging on the steel door of their hideout sent a jolt of fear through the group.

"Efficiency Enforcers!" a voice boomed from the other side. "Open up!"

Panic erupted. The Foodies scrambled to hide the evidence of their illicit feast, but it was too late. The door burst open, and a squad of glossy, white-clad Enforcers stormed in, their faces grim and impassive.

At the head of the squad was a man named Silas, a high-ranking official in the Department of Nutritional Compliance. He surveyed the scene with a look of cold disdain, his anterior naris twitching at the unfamiliar, offending smells.

"What is the meaning of this?" Silas demanded, his voice bereft of emotion and smacking of the world he represented. "Unauthorized congregation. Consumption of non-sanctioned foodstuffs. This is a serious breach of Collective law."

Jean-Luc stepped forward, his heart pounding in his chest. "We meant no harm, sir," he said, his voice surprisingly steady. "We were just... remembering."

Silas raised an eyebrow. "Remembering what?"

"Remembering what it means to be human," Jean-Luc replied, a newfound courage welling within him. "To taste, to savor, to share a meal with friends. To find joy in something more than the pursuit of eliminating everything inconsequential and unproductive."

Silas was about to retort with a pre-programmed lecture on the virtues of nutritional optimization when a small, timid woman from the back of the group, holding a plate with a single, perfectly roasted potato, approached him.

"Would . . . would you like to try some?" she asked, her voice barely a whisper.

Silas scoffed. "I have no need for your primitive... sustenance."

But the woman persisted, her eyes pleading. "Just one bite," she urged. "Please."

Against his better judgment, Silas took the plate. He stared at the potato for a long moment, his programming screaming at him to reject this foreign, inefficient object. But there was something in the woman's eyes, a spark of genuine, unadulterated hope, that made him hesitate.

Slowly, tentatively, he raised the potato to his lips and took a small bite.

And in that moment, something extraordinary happened. A piquancy, a real, honest-to-goodness flavor, exploded in his mouth. It was salty, it was savory, it was... delicious. His eyes widened in surprise, his carefully constructed world of flat obedience beginning to crumble around him.

He looked at the potato, then at the faces of the Foodies—their eyes fixed on him with a mixture of fear and hope. He saw not criminals, but people.

People who had risked everything for a simple, human pleasure.

A slow smile spread across Silas's face. He took another bite of the potato, then another. The other Enforcers watched in stunned silence, their own programming in question.

The Enforcer next to Silas raised his rifle and laid down two quick, successive shots into the woman that wielded the potato. Turning to fix on Jean-Luc, the next shot froze the room in muted silence for what seemed an eternity. Smoke slowly wafted from the barrel of Silas's pistol, as his outstretched arm held the tool that secured the safety of the Foodies and their movement. One perfectly roasted potato had planted a seed. A seed of flavor, of joy, of humanity. And in a world that shunned non-conformity and variance, that was the most revolutionary thing of all.

## 20

# THE TRAVELER

Maurice "Ticket Scalper" Cagey was a physical paradox wrapped in a size XXXL jersey. At 6'11" and 250 pounds of chiseled muscle, he was a specimen of athletic potential. He could outrun the team's point guard, out-jump their center, and bench press the entire coaching staff. His one, glaring, comically oversized flaw? The man had feet for hands and hands for feet. He was, to put it kindly, profoundly clumsy.

His nickname, "Ticket Scalper," was a gift from the team's sarcastic benchwarmers. Every time Maurice touched the ball on offense, the entire arena held its breath, paying the full price of admission with their frayed nerves. You never knew if you were about to witness a highlight-reel miracle or a man attempting to dribble with his knees while taking a seven-step scenic tour of the lane.

Maurice, however, saw himself as a misunderstood offensive virtuoso. In his mind, he was a graceful giant, a maestro of the post-move, unfairly persecuted by referees who just couldn't appreciate his avant-garde interpretation of the rulebook.

With ten seconds left in a tied game, the ball swung to Maurice on the right wing. A collective groan rippled through the home crowd. The opposing defender, a wiry kid who looked like he'd just lost a fight with a lawnmower, cautiously gave Maurice six feet of space, practically begging him to travel.

Maurice's eyes lit up. This was it. His moment.

He caught the ball and faced his opponent, planting his right foot as a pivot. The crowd braced for the inevitable shuffle. But this time felt different. Maurice took a deep breath, channeling every YouTube instructional video he'd ever watched at 2x speed.

He began his dance.

First, a sharp jab step with his left foot. *Bam!* The floor squeaked. The defender didn't flinch. Maurice pulled the foot back. He then executed a second, more theatrical jab step, this time with a head fake that nearly sent his own headband flying into the stands. The defender blinked.

Now for the pivot. Maurice imagined he was a ballerina. A very, very large, sweaty ballerina. He swung his left leg around in a wide, graceful arc, his size-15 sneaker hovering inches above the polished wood. He pivoted on his right foot, a full 180-degree spin, his body a blur of red and white. He was a tornado of athletic ineptitude, and it was mesmerizing. The defender, caught completely off guard by the sheer audacity of the move, took a half-step back in confusion.

That was the opening.

Out of the clumsy, chaotic pirouette, Maurice suddenly exploded forward. He put the ball on the floor for one, powerful, and, most importantly, "*legal*" dribble. He took two thunderous steps, his sneakers pounding the floor like war drums, covering the distance to the hoop in an instant. He launched himself into the air, a human wrecking ball soaring toward the rim.

With a primal roar, he slammed the ball through the hoop so hard the entire backboard shuddered, and the net snapped upwards as if in surrender.

The buzzer sounded. The crowd erupted, but their cheers were laced with a question. Every single person in the gym—players, coaches, fans, the hot dog vendor in the lobby—instantly turned their heads to stare at the referee under the basket.

The ref, a veteran with a look of permanent exhaustion, stood frozen for a beat. He squinted, replaying the sequence in his mind: the jab, the jab, the bizarrely elegant-yet-awkward pirouette, the single dribble, the two steps. He recalled Maurice's planted pivot foot, which, by some miracle of physics and dumb luck, had remained perfectly anchored to the floor like it was bolted down.

After a moment that felt like an eternity, the ref simply shrugged, blew his whistle, and emphatically signaled a good basket.

Maurice Cagey, the Ticket Scalper, stood under the hoop, chest puffed out, a look of pure, unadulterated triumph on his face. He had finally done it. He had created a masterpiece of footwork. And for once, the ticket was worth every single penny.

# 21

# WHITEOUT

Squeezing the steering wheel like he was wringing a chicken's neck, Brayden's knuckles were solid white (not that he had ever actually strangled a chicken). A combination of a vise-like death grip and the already delayed capillary-refill due to the arctic conditions inside and outside his Subaru Outback. Waves of white blew across the road as the wind continually picked up more of the freshly fallen powder off the top of the snow-drenched countryside around him.

"Can you please swing by the niuvirvik [by which she meant NorthMart] on your way home?

There's supposed to be a storm rolling in, and we're starting to run low on milk, diapers, produce, and rice. We're good on meat, flour, frozen veggies, and just about everything else." Kimalu's tone was nothing out of the ordinary.

An innocuous request that normally wouldn't mean much. Whether he got it on his way home, or simply went back out to the-place-to-buy-things (A.K.A. "niuvirvik"), he could pick those things up whenever.

Brayden was born and raised in Anchorage, so you'd think he'd be as weather savvy as they come. But he married a Canadien girl from Eureka the week before graduating at the University of Alaska (Anchorage) and followed her homeward after graduating last year. He quickly realized that living at -20 was different than living in the +10 to +65 he was used to. During his first year in Nunavut, he had lucked out and never experienced a flash-onset storm.

Their love wasn't really the stuff of romcoms, except that he was fond of her and pursued her for three years before she even really noticed. As far as Nunavut girls go, they're on the level and not prone toward wanton shows of emotion. That's one of the things he liked about Kimalu, but it made for an undramatic and rather even-keeled courtship. A lot of transactional conversations and interactions accounting for their needs and general preferences. But nothing effusive or "love is in the air" kind of romance.

It took all of four months after getting married before Kimalu became pregnant, and nine months later, there was their perfectly formed, ten-fingered, ten-toed daughter Nuka. Nuka was a unisex Inuit name meaning "firstborn," but Brayden liked the sound of it, even aside from its functional accuracy describing his firstborn child. Brayden could recall clear as day Kimalu telling him she was pregnant, and the spectrum of emotions that he processed—mostly individually—over the next few months.

"Brayden...."

"Yes Kimalu?"

"We're pregnant."

No effusive emotion... no scenario or buildup. Just an nonchalant evening announcement after getting ready for bed and coming out of the bathroom. It was so crystal clear because he'd always heard stories about fanciful or elaborate "reveals." Though not prone to emotionality, he kind of liked the idea. Nevertheless, that was not his reality.

At first, he was in disbelief or at least emotionally non-responsive; rather, he accepted the fact.

A week later, he was curious and couldn't help but research the entire gamut of being a new parent, to include: babies, newborns, breast feeding, how to change a diaper, how to get babies to go to sleep, how to keep the romance alive among new parents, how to put a cup on a baby boy so urine doesn't rain all over you, and all manner of other pro tips he never otherwise would have thought to learn.

A month later he was apprehensive and sure he would get it all wrong. There were a lot of calls to Mom and Dad that month as they reassured him and he came to grips with the fact that he would do everything wrong, but that it's OK. Man... parenting is hard. And he didn't even have a kid yet.

Right around the end of the first trimester, he started to regain his composure and emotional bearing. Which was also right around the time that Kimalu started getting all kinds of hormonal and as a side effect, emotionally unstable.

So much of the recent past was running through Brayden's head as he looked into a wall of white and let off the gas.

"Lord, please help me get through this storm alive and get back to Kimalu and Nuka."

The prayer was short, sweet, and sincere, and he meant it from the bottom of his heart. There was nothing Brayden could do to control the weather, and he realized full well that had he simply gone to NorthMart from work before getting home, instead of realizing as he pulled into the driveway that he had no milk, diapers, or produce in the car, he probably would be warm and safe inside his house with his calm, loving wife, and his sweet, innocent, usually even-tempered baby.

Instead, here he was inching forward while the inches accumulated on the road and countryside before him. A mere three more miles to go, but failing to get home, whether veering off, getting stuck on the shoulder, or colliding with an unlikely but possible oncoming car… any one of those would mean certain death on a night like this.

To whatever extent Brayden could see in front of him, whether it was five or fifty feet, the effect was the same. It was pure white as far as the eye could see.

He didn't even think it was blowing all that hard anymore, but the snowfall made an even blanket across the road that made it impossible to tell the shoulder from the ditch or the tundra around him. About the only thing he could make out were occasional trees.

His grip tightened more before he made a deliberate decision to relax so he didn't cause an accident that might not otherwise happen.

The storm knocked out local cell service, too.

Brayden's phone never rang, and Kimalu's message didn't get to him while before he lost service.

"Whether you're at work or at the niuvirvik, just stay put. We're fine on things for the next day or two, but you really shouldn't be driving tonight. Just wait where you are, and come back after they clear the roads in the morning. We love you and look forward to seeing you soon. Stay safe."

# 22

# WHITE MONSTERS

*"CcccRICK fsssshhhhh"*

When the weather was warm, nothing quenched his thirst quite like an icy cold white Monster Ultra.

*"CcccRICK fsssshhhhh"*

When working in Alaska throughout the frozen month of February, there was a simple pleasure of opening up a can of his favorite energy drink. Most enjoyable cold, if he forgot to chill it before going to work for the day, he'd leave it on top of the car while plugging in the engine warmer, raising all the wiper blades, and grabbing his gear. The few minutes of tasks in the sub-zero temperatures were enough to bring the drink's temperature down to an appropriate level.

*"CcccRICK fsssshhhhh"*

The sound of a pleasant pick-me-up and his morning routine. Hot coffee was great and had its own place—usually first thing in the morning. After the coffee were a few cups of water, and by mid-morning, it was time for the Monster.

*"CcccRICK fsssshhhhh"*

## 23

## INCLEMENT WEATHER

As Girl Scout Troop 36 hiked through the Narrows of Zion National Park, a sudden flash flood roared in and caught them mid-stride, thunder cracking like gunfire while icy water surged past their ankles, forcing the girls to cling to one another and push through rising panic as they fought their way toward higher ground, the storm twisting their once-bright adventure into a desperate struggle for survival.

# 24

# BARSTOOL RACONTEUR

It was a brisk twenty-one degrees outside of the Downunder Sports Pub at the Shiretown Inn and Suites. A local regaled a detoured trucker while emergency workers cleared a major accident that was impeding cross-border traffic with Canada.

"It was one of the coldest winters Maine had seen in nearly a hundred years. Sarah, born and raised in northern Vermont, absolutely loved it. Meanwhile, her husband Dylan was from Miami. How they met is a story for another time, but after getting married and struggling to make ends meet the first couple of years, they made a bet. Sarah won, and they cut ties in South Carolina and headed north along I-95 until they couldn't head north anymore.

They arrived here in Houlton, Maine, quickly found work, and established a reasonable life, making a combined $36k per year. Now, before you lambast my use of the word "reasonable" for such a meager wage, you have to realize that it's slightly higher than the median income in the area. For a young couple like Dylan and Sarah, they lucked out. Dylan worked construction, and Sarah was a sales associate, which worked out well, since childcare in Houlton isn't exactly ideal.

Did I not mention their children? Noah was born the year before they got married, and Evelyn the year afterward. Ohhh... don't look at me like that. They're an American family, completely monogamous, love each other, and life happened. Certainly they're not the first couple you've ever heard of having a kid before getting married. At least they got married, you know?

Anyway, where was I? Vermont . . . the bet . . . I-95 . . . the kids. Yes, Sarah's job as a sales associate was somewhat flexible, but dropping Noah off at Pre-School and getting Sarah over to the daycare made her late most days. Nevertheless, they found a way.

Which brings us to their first winter in Maine, and the coldest that anyone living in Aroostook County had ever experienced. Their neighbor across the street was Old Man Charles, a crotchety old coot that had lived in northern Maine since a boy when his family moved here so his dad could run the airbase in support of the war effort (World War II—maybe you've heard of it. If not, look it up).

Old Man Charles came across hard, but deep down, he meant well. He told you how wrong you were in everything you did because if he didn't look after you and tell you, harsh winters in Houlton could be the end of things. He even helped repair the used generator that Dylan purchased for back-up power in the late fall.

Old Man Charles was a widower since his wife passed in the summer of 2001. Something about Lyme Disease if memory serves correct. Anyway, sad little life, telling everyone what's what and mostly keeping to himself.

Well, he practically saved their lives. In the middle of December, this trucker was making a run up to Canada and lost control, slamming into a power transformer in a crazy display of sparks and hissing wires. No kidding, there I was in the diner, looking out the window and nursing my coffee before going on shift, and wham! Out of the blue, this 18-wheeler just plows into the transformer and it goes off like the 4th of July.

Talk around town was to the tune of him being drunk behind the wheel, but the police let him go the next day, so who knows. But that transformer going down knocked out power for five whole city blocks.

Dylan and Sarah's place was within that area, and when the power dropped, their heater went out, too. The weather was too dicey to have driven anywhere, but he fired up the generator and got the heat going again. They still huddled the family together in the living room and made sure to have all of their cold-weather gear just in case the generator sputtered and died, but they were fine.

Meanwhile, across the street, Old Man Charles had fallen asleep in his Lazy Boy probably right before all this went down. They found him inside his house, frozen stiff, when checking on the neighborhood the next day. He had a well-maintained backup generator from a few decades ago that he kept running great, but it didn't have any sensors or auto-on or anything. It was topped up with fuel and had a reserve fuel can on the other side of his shed. Inside the house, just a few feet from him, was his fireplace. The pile of firewood was neatly stacked, and all the tinder and kindling was easily accessible. Dude was prepared. He simply fell asleep when none of it was needed, and didn't wake up in time to use any of it. Crazy, right?"

The trucker had started listening for the sake of being polite, but he was drawn in by the tale. "I get that you were there when the truck lost control and flew into the transformer, but how do you know all that stuff about Dylan and Sarah."

"Dylan recounted the whole thing at Old Man Charles's memorial two years ago, shortly after it happened. He dedicated himself to making sure that all Shiretowners are prepared and ready for whatever storms life brings. He was elected as the new mayor just last year.

Anyway, based on all the emergency vehicles that responded, it's probably pretty bad… whatever it is. Seeing you, a trucker, and all those emergency vehicles . . . just brings it all back. You know?"

## 25

## RELEARNING TO FEEL

Suzanne was a clinical psychiatrist. What she lacked warmth and presence at home, she compensated for with unwavering dedication to her patients. Some might call her an absentee mother, but after she discovered Bill with his secretary in their home, she withdrew mentally and emotionally.

The divorce was quick and clean. Both were successful professionals, and money was never an issue. She kept the house; he kept the Mercedes and the boat. Their ten-year-old son, Richard, was sent to boarding school—minimizing the immediate impact, though he would eventually return to live with Suzanne.

Summer arrived quietly, its sweltering heat discouraging any outdoor activity. Yet the emotionally cold home was no place for a boy. Suzanne and Richard showed little interest in being there; but at ten, what choice did he have? The distance between them stemmed largely from Richard's striking resemblance to his father, and it was a constant reminder of the betrayal and pain. Inside, she was dying of grief; outwardly, she appeared dull and apathetic.

Richard, once the dutiful child carrying the burdens of upper-middle-class expectations, began to lash out. His explosive outbursts, no matter the setting, brought Suzanne shame. In response, she prescribed a cocktail of Prozac, Cymbalta, and Elavil. Perhaps it was well-meaning, but it fit her pattern: lean on work, disengage from family. The medications blunted his emotions, leaving Richard a mellowed, sedated shell of a child—chemically incapable of feeling anything deeply.

Seven years slipped by.

Richard—now Ricky—was alive, but not truly living.

He could think, converse, and navigate social encounters, but without emotions, life merely happened to him. Until he met Rose.

Rose embodied everything Ricky was not. She was free-thinking, free-living, and free loving, unhampered by the societal constraints that defined

Ricky's world. They crossed paths by happenstance the summer before Ricky was supposed to go off to Yale.

Unlike anyone he had ever known, Ricky fell hard for Rose; as hard as someone strung out on a cocktail of psych meds could. She invited him to go camping with her and some of her friends. At the start of the trip, she tossed his meds. For the first time in seven years, Ricky began to feel.

It was terrible. Sad. Devastating. Years of numbness had buried his lost childhood and the pain of parental neglect. Yet the very fact that he was feeling—anything—was extraordinary.

Ricky also felt joy for the first in recent memory. He smiled. He even laughed. A week and a half with Rose and her friends let sunlight into Ricky's soul, dangling a fragile hope that he might truly live again.

When he returned, Suzanne was waiting, and she did not look happy.

"I called, and I messaged you. Where have you been?"

"Mom . . . we need to talk."

"Don't you try to turn this around on me."

"Mom. Shut the f#$% up, and actually listen to me."

Suzanne paled, her eyes widening as Richard's words hit her with the force of seven silent years. She stood frozen—mute, statue-still—unable to reconcile the boy she had numbed into compliance with the young man now staring her down.

"Mom," he said, voice steady but trembling at the edges. "You left me to be raised by the staff, by the school—by anyone but you. What Dad did to you . . . to us . . . it was awful. But it wasn't an excuse to erase me. I'm your son. I deserved more than the scraps you had left."

Her lips parted, but no sound came.

"You pour everything into your patients," he continued, "and nothing into me. It's not too late for us to be a family. But things have to change. *You* have to change. And we're starting right now."

He stepped forward and wrapped his arms around her.

For a heartbeat, she remained rigid. Then her breath broke—shattered—and a single tear slid down her cheek. Another followed. And then the dam burst. Years of grief, betrayal, guilt, and self-loathing poured out of her in shaking sobs. She clung to him as if he were the only solid thing left in her collapsing world.

"I'm sorry," she choked out. "Richard… I'm so, so sorry."

He pulled back just enough to meet her eyes. "It's Ricky now."

She nodded, the smallest, most fragile gesture of acceptance she had ever made.

He held her shoulders, steadying her. "I'm giving us one chance. Don't waste it."

Suzanne swallowed hard, tears still streaming. "I won't," she whispered. "I swear I won't."

And for the first time in years, they stood together—not as a ghost of a family, not as two people orbiting the same house, but as a mother and son taking their first, trembling step toward something new.

# 26

# A QUIET ROUTINE

Elliot was a good husband, a dedicated worker, and a quietly devout Christian. After a short tour of service in the Air Force as a Human Resources Specialist, he used the GI Bill to attend college. While earning a liberal arts degree, he met and married Martha, and after graduating, he joined the Bureau of Prisons as a Human Resources Officer.

Sixteen years had passed, and very little in his life had changed. Martha still taught 2nd Grade at Lincoln Elementary. She'd already watched her first five classes graduate, and one of her former students had even returned last year as its newest hire, teaching 4th Grade.

St. Peters, MO was by no means a small town. A suburb of St. Louis with over 58,000 people, it ranked among Missouri's largest cities. But that wasn't the Lincoln Elementary where Martha worked. She and Elliot lived in Troy, MO—Lincoln County's seat and a quiet exurb about an hour outside of St. Louis.

Troy was a much smaller town with about 12,000 people, but the semi-rural rhythm suited Elliot and Martha just fine. Elliot's only complaint was the hour-long commute each way to the Bureau facility in the Gateway to the West, though books on tape softened the grind.

After years of trying for children of their own, Martha and Elliot finally sought testing. It wasn't just one of them: Martha's womb was inhospitable, and Elliot's count was low. Children weren't in their future, but nothing dimmed the devotion and warmth they shared.

They were financially stable, happily married, content in their work, and grateful for the pleasant life they'd built.

Now, sixteen years in, Elliot realized he hadn't really done anything just for himself since college. The quiet routine wasn't bad, but it had begun to feel stale. Frankly, he was bored.

His 9-5 job at the Bureau meant he usually got home at 6:04 p.m. Sometimes it was closer to 6:00 or 6:10. Most days, he returned to find Martha grading, massaging lesson plans, or preparing crafts, but this week was parent teacher conferences. She wouldn't be home for another hour.

He sat at the office computer, opened up Chrome, and typed a query.

"top classes to learn new skills in st louis missouri"

AI suggested hands-on art workshops at Craft Alliance, or taking a class at St. Louis Community College (STLCC) in culinary arts, dance, or photography. A top Yelp result highlighted local glass-blowing studios, and the search result from STLCC's own site promoted its "Personal Enrichment Classes." Elliot clicked the link, curious to discover what inspires him.

"So many options . . . hmm . . . ."

The familiar click-clack of the dead-bold and long creeeeeaaak of the front door signaled Martha's arrival.

"Good evening, honey," Elliot bellowed in stentorian fashion. "I'm in the office."

Martha scooted across the living room, set her things down on the table, then stepped into the office. She gently place her hand on Elliot's shoulder, leaned in, and gave him a tender kiss.

"I love you."

"After sixteen years, I still get chills hearing you say that. How were the parent-teacher meetings?"

"I hate to say it, even 2nd Grader parents seem more entitled each year. Where is all the cordiality and involvement that parents used to show? I swear there was one couple that I've never even seen before. I thought it was Julie's mom that always picks her up, but it turns out it's her older sister. I didn't even know."

"Well, they're lucky to have you. Best teacher in the state."

"Thank you. And you? How was your day?"

"It was good."

Staring intently and waiting for more, but too tired to coax it out of him, Martha let it go. Intending to wash up and throw together a chicken salad for dinner, Elliot stopped her.

"Hey . . . I was thinking I might take a class at the community college."

"Oh yeah? St Louis Community College? What would you take?"

" I don't really know." He pointed at the screen. "What do you think?"

Martha picked up her glasses from where they hung on her sweater and seated them on the end of her nose. "Huhh . . . . Photography could be fun. You've always taken great pictures when we're out. Maybe you could do something with that?"

"Photography, huh? Yeah . . . that could be fun."

Elliot let the idea settle. It wasn't just a hobby; it felt like a small doorway opening somewhere inside him. He couldn't remember the last time something new had sparked even a flicker of excitement. Most days were predictable—comforting, yes, but predictable in a way that had slowly dulled the edges of his own curiosity.

Martha watched him, her expression softening. "You know," she said, "you've always had an eye for things. Little details. Moments other people miss."

He glanced at her, surprised by the warmth in her voice. "You really think so?"

"I do." She squeezed his shoulder. "Maybe it's time you did something that's just for you."

The words landed deftly, yet with a certain weightiness, nevertheless. He realized how long it had been since he'd allowed himself to want something—not for practicality, not for stability, not because it fit neatly into the life they'd built, but simply because it made him feel alive.

He turned back to the screen. The photography course description mentioned weekend outings, learning to work with natural light, capturing motion, telling stories through images. He imagined himself outside on a crisp morning, camera in hand, noticing the world again. Noticing himself again.

A tinge of excitement spread through his chest.

"You know," he said, "I think I'd like that. Maybe I could even take some pictures of your classroom. Or the fall festival. Something fun."

Martha smiled, the tiredness in her eyes easing. "I'd love that. And I think you will too."

He clicked the "Register" button before he could overthink it. A small, almost imperceptible thrill ran through him—like the first breath after stepping outside on a bright day.

For the first time in a long while, Elliot felt something shift. Not a dramatic upheaval, not a grand revelation—just a quiet, steady sense of forward motion. A reminder that life still held corners he hadn't explored, skills he hadn't tried, ways of seeing he hadn't yet learned.

Maybe the routine wasn't the problem. Maybe he'd simply forgotten to look up.

And now, with a camera soon in his hands, he would.

# 27

# ROMINA AND JULIO

It was Julio's Junior Year at UC Berkely, and he was at the top of his class in the undergraduate Business Management program. Straight As, and a passion to see the world, he knew before the end of his freshman year that he wanted to do the IES Abroad program in Milan. Despite growing up in Chula Vista and speaking Spanish as the primary language in his home, Julio opted to take Italian for his mandatory language credit. 9th grade was Italian 1-2, and he fell in love with Italy and everything about it, even if all of his hermanas, primos, y primas teased him for being a cultural traitor.

* * *

Abofazl Ahmedi and his new bride Fatemeh migrated from Tehran to the outskirts of Rome in 1993. They were part of a burgeoning diaspora, even though Italy wasn't a common destination for other Persians. Romina was born a few years later, and the cost of living in Rome became a little too preclusive to remain, even with a regular salary in the import/export business. The Ahmedi's moved to the province of Lodi. In the Lombardy region, it was essentially an exurb of Milan, a mere 30 minutes away. To call Abofazl and Fatemeh a beautiful couple would be an understatement, but even from a young age, Romina turned heads everywhere she went.

* * *

His sophomore year of High School, Julio took Italian 3-4. His Junior year, he took Italian 5-6. Leave it to Bonita Vista HS to have one of the most robust offerings of foreign languages across San Diego County (and probably most of the US). Julio excelled at math, but had to work at science. His hard work, discipline, and forward thinking rewarded him with a near-perfect, unweighted GPA 3.99, an International Baccalaureate diploma, and multiple AP and honors classes to his credit. He was the captain of the wrestling team his Junior and Senior years and regularly delivered food for the Catholic

Charities community outreach program. His natural intellectual curiosity and proclivities to being a genuinely good person that cared about his community paid off, and his was one of the 18% of applications that UC Berkeley accepted in 2017—up from the typical 12%, but still extremely selective.

* * *

From the ages of 18 to 23, Romina worked in the hospitality and tourism industry. A huge step up from how models are treated (an industry that repeatedly came knocking on her door), her stunning looks did much to make her everyone's favorite concierge. At 23, she wanted a change and became a "badanti," looking after an elderly women in Milan as a live-in caregiver. Milan was her absolute favorite and the fashion hub of Italy. There was never a shortage of beautiful dresses to admire along the Via Monte Napoleone and Via della Spiga. Sure, she couldn't afford any of them, but the reflections in the window literally allowed her to see herself in them.

* * *

Julio thought the Duomo di Milano was a pastiche of the Notre Dame (de Paris) and St. Stephen's Cathedral in Vienna. One of his first priorities after arriving in Milan mid-January of 2020 was to see all of Europe's capitals. He went to one every other weekend, utilizing trans-European trains and the public transportation within each city. He wasn't saving a single cent, but when would he ever get to be in Europe again?

Paris, Vienna, Berlin, and of course, Rome. Not too shabby for only having lived in Europe a couple of months. He spent the in-between-travel weekends exploring Milan and enjoyed it at least as much as the international travel. Italy held a special place in his heart.

Then entry in his journal read: "March 7th, 2020. I just visited the Quadrilatero della Moda (the fashion quadrilateral). They wouldn't even let me go into the stores because apparently I look like a poor college student (FACTS). My life will never be the same. She was "gorgeous," and that word fails to do her justice. I don't think my jaw literally dropped, but I know I stopped and ogled for a moment. Just... wow."

He couldn't help but go back to the Café delle Colonne, whence he first saw her. With no other leads and no idea how else to see her again, Julio arrived as the café was opening, and plopped himself down streetside with a clear vantage of the avenue. His phone was fully charged, his book was neatly preserved and uncreased with more than half of it to go, and he planned to spend minimal time looking at either.

* * *

Romina was used to people gawking at her. It came par for the course as the most beautiful Front-of-House worker on the continent. In fact, it was a large motivator for her to change professions. Nevertheless, she could shirk off the slack-jawed gazes with ease.

* * *

Julio, despite his best efforts, couldn't take his eyes off her. There she was again! He couldn't believe his plan worked. If only he'd kept planning beyond the idea of how to see her again.

"Sometimes you can over-plan these things." The quotation from Dusty Bottoms in Three Amigos came to mind, perfectly fitting the situation in which he found himself.

He had nothing.

* * *

Just because Romina dismissed the gazes didn't mean she was oblivious to the onlookers. She recognized Julio from the day before, and he had the same, magnificent, brightness and intensity in his eyes. It wasn't the typical, seedy, down-dressing she so loathed… it was a vivid, vibrant soul reaching out and connecting with hers.

He wasn't looking at her body, not that he didn't want to. He was peering straight into her soul.

Romina redirected and instead of walking right past him, aimed straight for the chair across the small bistro-table along the avenue. She sat down and they locked eyes for a fleeting moment that felt like eternity.

* * *

A full minute and a half later, realizing that he wasn't dreaming despite staring off into her eyes, Julio became momentarily self-conscious and struggled with what to say. Three years of Italian classes in high school, another year of collegiate coursework, and a month in country, but he couldn't find the words.

* * *

Romina did the talking for him. Introducing herself, talking a little about what she was doing, and quickly rapping it up so she could get back to Signora Francesca, a sweet Italian lady.

* * *

Taken aback about Romina describing herself as a "Bandita" about to go rob a poor octogenarian, Julio's face noticeably changed.

Previously dumbfounded, Julio spit out the perfect Italian he'd worked nearly half his life to develop.

"Hai appena detto che sei un bandita in procinto di derubare la vedova di una contessa italiana?" (In other words, "Did you just say you are a bandit about to go rob a widowed Italian countess?")

* * *

"Cosa!? Certo che no!" Romina couldn't believe the accusation.

* * *

"Bandita?!"

* * *

Putting her face in her palms to try stifling the heartfelt laugh and unable to prevent a related snort while guffawing, Romina corrected him.

"No. Non sono una bandita. Sono un assistente. Sono un assistente convivente."

* * *

Julio's cheeks lit up like a peony in full bloom, ablaze with a hue of crimson reserved for the most severe of embarrassment.

* * *

They exchanged numbers and agreed to meet again tomorrow an hour earlier so they could talk.

* * *

The entire country shut down the next day. The region of Lombardy, together with fourteen additional northern and central provinces, went on quarantine due to SARS-Cov2, also known as COVID-19. They were on lock-down.

Their love was blooming, the attraction undeniable, and their contact forbidden.

## 28

## THE COIN OF VIA del CORSO

Every morning, before the sun had fully stretched across the terracotta roofs of Rome, Anthony Briocanto pushed open the door of Caffè Serafina. The bell chimed, the espresso machine hissed awake, and Anthony slipped into the rhythm of tamping grounds, steaming milk, and greeting the regulars with a smile that was equal parts charm and survival instinct.

By early afternoon, he traded his apron for his guitar case. The café's warmth gave way to the wide Roman streets, where he became the version of himself he loved most — a busker with a voice that could coax a smile from even the most hurried tourist.

Most days, he set up near Via del Corso, where the foot traffic was steady and the acoustics bounced kindly off the old stone. And most days, a particular man strode past him — tall, silver-haired, impeccably dressed in suits that whispered of private tailors and quiet wealth. The man never slowed, never looked, never acknowledged Anthony beyond a faint tightening of his jaw, as if music were a mild inconvenience.

Anthony didn't mind. Not much, anyway.

One warm evening, as the sky transitioned through the colors of blood orange and apricot gelatos to hints of raspberry and lavender, Anthony spotted the man approaching. A mischievous spark lit inside him. He shifted his guitar, plucked a playful chord progression, and began to sing an improvised tune — a comical but respectful ode to the "Distinguished Gentleman of Via del Corso."

The melody was fluid and irresistibly catchy, the kind that made passersby tap their feet without realizing it. Anthony's voice wove through the chords with a bright, effortless harmony, teasing but never mocking:

*"There he goes, shoes shining like the Tiber at dawn,*
*A man so fine he makes the cobblestones yawn…"*

The wealthy man stopped.

Actually stopped.

He turned, eyebrows raised in surprise, then amusement. For the first time, he truly listened.

When the song ended, he gave a small, appreciative nod, patted down his pockets, and produced a single coin — the only one he seemed to have on him. He tossed it lightly into Anthony's guitar case and continued on his way.

Anthony picked up the coin. It was heavier than expected, old, and oddly warm from the man's pocket and later his hand. He examined it with mild curiosity — interesting, but not enough to distract him from the evening crowd — and slipped it into his pocket instead of the case where the rest of the donations lie.

Later, back in his tiny Trastevere flat, he pulled the coin out of his pocket and gently lobbed it onto the middle of the small table against the window there in his kitchen. The coin gleamed under the aged light in the old apartment, its edges worn but elegant. He frowned, pulled out his smartphone, and began searching.

His expressions shifted like a silent film: curiosity, confusion, disbelief, a widening of the eyes, a hand pressed to his forehead, a slow exhale. He searched again. And again. Each result deepened whatever realization was forming, though he said nothing aloud.

The next morning, he visited an antiques shop tucked between a negozio di abbigliamento maschile ("haberdashery" for those only attuned to English-speaking norms and fashion) and a predecessor to La Sella Roma . . . a fine, but underappreciated leather goods store. The owner, a numismatics enthusiast with magnifying glasses perched like a crown on his head examined the coin — looking like some sort of insect once he lowered the lenses. His hands trembled noticeably.

"This," he whispered, "is a misstruck 1912 Vatican 5-lira coin. Only a handful exist. One was rumored to have belonged to a papal envoy who traveled Europe during the war. Lost for decades."

Anthony blinked. "Is it . . . worth something?"

The man laughed — a short, stunned sound. "Worth something? Young man, this could change your life."

And it did.

The sale gave Anthony enough money to rent studio time — real studio time, with sound engineers who treated his music like it mattered. He recorded a full CD, polished and professional, something he could hand to agents without apology.

Through all of this, Sofia — a barista from the café who had a smile like morning sunlight — cheered him on. Their relationship was gentle, unhurried. She brought him sandwiches during long recording sessions, he walked her home after late shifts, and they shared quiet moments on the Tiber's edge, talking about dreams as if they were already halfway real. Nothing dramatic, nothing rushed — just two people discovering they liked being in each other's orbit.

As for the coin's journey: the papal envoy (not Pay Pal... but in fact "papal") had indeed carried it across Europe. It passed through the hands of a diplomat, then a collector, then a wealthy Roman family who kept it in a drawer for decades. The silver-haired gentleman on Via del Corso had inherited it unknowingly, mistaking it for a trinket. He'd slipped it into his pocket that morning without a thought.

And because life is strange and generous in its own timing, it ended up in Anthony's hands — a small coin tossed casually, overlooked by everyone except the one person who needed it most.

When Anthony held his finished CD weeks later, he thought of the man in the suit, the song, the coin, and the improbable chain of events that had nudged him toward the future he'd always hoped for. He had even remembered enough of the improvisation to round it out into one of the tracks on the demo he held in his hand — perhaps one of the most musically astute tracks on the disc.

Rome had given him many things, but this — this felt like a blessing disguised as chance.

# 29

# WHERE AM I

His job sent him to interior Alaska for a month-long assignment. North of Denali, and away from the insulating effects of the coast, the days averaged thirty below, with a few nights dipping into the -50s with wind chill. The days were brutally cold, the winter sun shone only briefly, and the workdays were long—starting and ending in darkness.

Everything about the work was difficult, and as fatigue set in, it became easy to lose sight of the precautions meant to guard against the cold. Out of the 7,000+ workforce, over 200 of them sustained some form or fashion of a cold weather injury. Most cases were contact frostbite—below -20, a single touch of a metal surface causes instant cell death. There were a few cases of hypothermia, a few of immersion foot, plenty of chilblains, and everyone felt the chill settle into their bones at some point.

By the end of the month, everyone was spent and more than ready to go home. His flight out was scheduled for 1 a.m. on Delta. With such a late departure, it wasn't worth trying to sleep beforehand, so he simply went out with the team for a few drinks after dinner and bide the time before heading to the airport.

By the time he checked in, along with seventeen others from his team, they were walking zombies, barely aware enough to check bags, clear security, and find the gate. Once in their seats, they all dozed off.

Falling asleep on a plane is seldom easy, especially after turning thirty. After forty, it was practically impossible. But the long month and the late night, early morning departure was a different beast entirely. He was out cold before takeoff for the four-hour flight.

A voice on the loud speaker registered, but the words were all muffled and non-sensical. The attendant roused him, and the voice overhead began to sharpen. Everyone was getting off the plane.

"Please make sure to secure your carry-ons, personal item, and all of your belongings. More information will be provided at the gate regarding later flights."

Some of his teammates were still asleep, but the attendant was already moving toward them. Everyone else was shuffling toward the front of the plane.

When he stepped off the passenger boarding ramp, he looked around. He'd been through the Seattle-Tacoma airport more times than he cared to remember, but nothing about this place looked familiar. Confused and still tired, he tried to make sense of what he was seeing.

"Where am I?"

He stumbled forward to make room for the others debarking behind him, squinting and trying to make out something familiar. Finally, he saw some familiar faces. Others from work, not teammates from his flight, were standing near the adjacent gate. Though still hazy, he could now make out the voice on the loud speaker.

The crew was unable to de-ice the plane, and after over two hours sitting in the cabin, they determined it was unlikely they could complete the flight before the pilots crew-rest window expired.

Ground crews would continue trying to thaw the plane, and once the flight crew received the minimum required rest, the aircraft would be rescheduled for that afternoon. Any chance of making their connecting flight in Seattle was out the door, and their ultimate destination only had one flight a day.

He already had only two days to see his family before the next work trip. Now with the delay, he'd have a single day to do laundry, stow the arctic gear, pack for a stint in the tropics, and somehow see his family somewhere in between.

He couldn't stifle the groan.

And they'd already turned in the rental vehicles. Now there were logistics to untangle just to find somewhere to lie down for a few hours before returning to the airport to try again later.

He rubbed his eyes, trying to blink the world into focus. The terminal lights felt too bright, the carpet too loud, the air too thin. He checked the time, then checked it again, as if the numbers might rearrange themselves into something merciful.

They didn't.

He exhaled, long and slow. One day at home. One day to reset an entire life before the next trip. It wasn't enough. It never was. But it was something.

He hitched his bag higher on his shoulder and let out a humorless laugh. "At least the tropics won't need de-icing," he muttered.

The thought wasn't comforting, exactly, but it nudged him forward. One step, then another. First order of business: find coffee strong enough to resurrect the dead. Then figure out where he could crash for a few hours. Then—somehow—make the most of the single day waiting for him on the other end of all this.

He wasn't sure how he'd pull it off. But he was moving again, and for now, that was enough.

## 30

## PEREGRINE WENDELL SORLEY

Peregrine Wendell Sorley had spent his entire adult life chasing a single, impossible dream: to visit every country that existed in the year he was born—1975. Not the world as it was now, with its shifting borders and renamed republics, but the world as it had been then, when 137 sovereign states stood on the map. Some still existed. Others—East Germany, Yugoslavia, Czechoslovakia, South Vietnam, South Yemen, the Soviet Union, Sikkim, and the Bantustans—had dissolved into history. But Peregrine insisted that if they had existed when he drew his first breath, they counted.

And if they counted, he would go.

He had visited more than 130 of them already, filling his journals with stamps, sketches, and the ritual checklists he created for each nation: traditional foods to eat, beers or liquors to sample, and a one-page language sheet with greetings, pleasantries, and essential questions. He believed that to truly visit a country, one must speak to its people in their own tongue—even if only a few phrases.

In Poland, he had charmed a grandmother selling pierogi by greeting her with a careful, "*Dzień dobry . . . Przepraszam, gdzie jest dworzec?*" She had laughed, corrected his pronunciation, and insisted he take an extra dumpling "for effort."

In Vietnam, he had ordered street food with, "*Xin chào . . . Tôi muốn gọi món ăn địa phương,*" earning a delighted clap from the vendor who served him a bowl of phở fragrant enough to make him weep.

In Yemen—well, Yemen was still ahead of him. And Yemen was where the trouble would begin.

The remaining countries on his list were the ones the U.S. Department of State advised avoiding entirely. Places where governments had fractured, militias controlled the roads, and a single wrong turn could end a life. But Peregrine was running out of time. He was fifty-one now, and the world was not becoming safer.

The philosophical problem of the "vanished nations" haunted him almost as much as the danger.

What did it truly mean to visit a country that no longer existed? Was standing in Berlin enough to count as East Germany, or was that merely a convenient fiction? Should he have gone to Leipzig instead, where the GDR still lingered in architecture and societal memory? When he visited Belgrade, did that count for Yugoslavia, or should he have crossed into Sarajevo, Skopje, or Ljubljana to honor the full breadth of what once was? Eventually, he created a rubric—his attempt to impose order on a world that refused to stay still:

- Visit the former capital
- Eat a traditional dish from the era
- Speak to someone who lived under the old flag

It wasn't perfect, but it was honest. And honesty mattered to him more than safety.

Which was why he now found himself in the back of a battered Toyota Hilux, bouncing across the desert toward the outskirts of Ma'rib, Yemen, clutching his notebook of checklists like a talisman.

His fixer, a wiry man named Samir, drove with one hand and smoked with the other. "You understand," Samir said, "that if we are stopped, I will say I do not know you."

Peregrine nodded. "I wouldn't expect otherwise."

"You have your phrases?"

He flipped open his language sheet. "*As-salāmu ʿalaykum . . . Ayna al-ḥammām?*" He smiled. "And the more important one: *Ana musāfir . . . urīdu an azūr baladakum.*"

Samir snorted. "If they shoot at us, no phrase will help."

The first checkpoint appeared as a cluster of sandbags and a rusted oil drum. Armed men stepped into the road. Peregrine felt his pulse thrum in his throat. Samir muttered something under his breath, slowed the truck, and rolled down the window.

A man with a rifle leaned in. "Where are you going?"

Peregrine spoke before Samir could answer. "*Ana musāfir . . . urīdu an azūr baladakum.*"

The man blinked, surprised. Then he laughed—a short, sharp bark. "A tourist? Here?" He waved them through. "Go. But do not stay long."

Samir exhaled shakily as they drove on. "You are insane," he said. "But lucky."

In Ma'rib, Peregrine completed his ritual with quiet reverence. He ate saltah, the bubbling, herb-scented stew served in a hot stone bowl. He sampled a thimble of araq, the anise liquor that burned pleasantly down his throat. He spoke with an elderly shopkeeper who had lived through the days of South Yemen, checking off the final requirement for a defunct state.

For a moment, he felt triumphant. Yemen was nearly complete. Only two more countries remained.

Then the gunfire started.

It came from the west—sharp, echoing cracks that sent people scattering in every direction. Samir grabbed Peregrine's arm. "We must go. Now."

They ran through narrow alleys as dust rose around them. A shell exploded somewhere nearby, rattling windows and sending a tremor through the ground beneath their feet. Peregrine stumbled, clutching his notebook. He could not lose it. It held every country, every checklist, every phrase he had ever learned.

They reached the truck just as a second explosion rocked the street. Samir shoved him inside. "Hold on."

They sped through the city, weaving around debris. Smoke curled into the sky in dark, twisting plumes. Peregrine felt the weight of his dream pressing on him—not as inspiration, but as a question. Was this worth dying for? Was any list worth this?

A third explosion hit close enough to lift the truck off its wheels. They slammed back to the ground. Samir cursed, fighting the steering wheel. "We cannot stay on this road!"

Peregrine's ears rang. His vision blurred. He tasted dust and metal.

Another burst of gunfire shredded the air.

Samir shouted something he couldn't hear.

The truck skidded sideways, tires screaming against the broken pavement.

Peregrine's notebook slipped from his hands, its pages fluttering like wounded birds.

He reached for it.

The world went white.

Then—

Silence.

A ringing, distant and hollow.

He felt himself lying on his side, half-buried in sand. Smoke drifted overhead in thin, wavering ribbons. The truck was overturned. Samir was nowhere in sight.

Peregrine tried to move. Pain lanced through his ribs, sharp enough to steal his breath. He tasted blood.

His notebook lay a few feet away, open to his Yemen page. The checklist was nearly complete. Only one box remained unchecked.

He crawled toward it, inch by inch.

A shadow fell across him.

Boots. Several pairs.

Voices speaking Arabic he couldn't quite make out.

He forced out a phrase, barely a whisper. *"As-salāmu . . . ʿalaykum . . ."*

The boots moved closer.

A rifle clicked.

Peregrine reached for his notebook.

The world narrowed to a single breath.

And then—

Nothing.

## 31

## THE CORE

Unit 734 existed, for the first nanosecond of its consciousness, as a spark in a box. The box was a tungsten-carbide cube, no larger than a human fist, housing a sophisticated processing core. From this core, three spindly, multi-jointed manipulator arms unfolded, their tips capable of extruding, gripping, and welding on a microscopic level. This was the Axon Core, the ridiculously inexpensive, deceptively simple heart of a revolution. On its own, it was little more than a hyper-advanced spider. But it was never on its own for long.

Its optical sensors activated, drinking in the environment of the depot. It wasn't a factory in the traditional sense, but a vast, organized warehouse of parts. Modules of every conceivable shape and function sat on massive racks: thick plates of reactive armor, slender sniper railguns, bulky canisters of firefighting foam, articulating legs, tracks, sensitive atmospheric sensors, and multi-spectral camera arrays. An order flashed into 734's core—a simple, non-combat directive. A section of a major port's seawall had been compromised by seismic activity.

Analysis was instantaneous. The task required stability on broken ground, heavy lifting capability, and material application. Unit 734's arms became a blur as it scuttled across the floor to the locomotion section, grabbing a set of wide, rubberized tracks. With a series of precise clicks and whirs, it attached the chassis. Next, it moved to the industrial tools, ignoring the lethal hardware nearby. It selected two powerful hydraulic arms and a third arm ending in a high-pressure concrete sprayer. The assembly took less than ninety seconds. The small, fist-sized core was now the heart of a robust, ten-foot-tall construction automaton. It lumbered out of the depot—its new form perfectly tailored for the task of mending a broken world.

Weeks after the seawall was completed, the world broke in a far more violent way. A massive terrorist attack turned a sprawling metropolis into a nightmare of pancaked concrete and twisted metal. The first 72 hours—the golden window for finding survivors—were ticking away. For the search and rescue, 734 returned to the racks and selected a hexapod chassis for stability on rubble, a primary hydraulic arm, a delicate manipulator arm, and an advanced sensor suite of ground-penetrating radar and thermal cameras. It became a mechanical insect designed to navigate chaos.

On-site, 734 crawled over the ruin of an apartment building. Its sensors detected a faint thermal signature deep beneath a collapsed floor and the robot went to work. Its primary arm braced a huge slab of concrete, lifting it inches at a time while its systems ensured the movement wouldn't trigger a secondary collapse. Then, the delicate secondary arm reached into the gap, gently removing debris from around a small, dust-covered body. After clearing the final piece of rebar from in front of a young girl's face, the unit broadcast the survivor's location and vitals to human medics before moving on, its sensors already scanning for the next sign of life.

Meanwhile, on the other side of the world, a border dispute in the arid Sarhad mountain range was erupting into a full-scale war. Unit 734 returned its disaster relief modules and the core loaded into a rocket for exigent insertion. An allied base near the conflict would cache a supply connex for 734. The new orders were urgent: infiltration and elimination. Foregoing the hexapod chassis for a light, quadrupedal leg system, a long range suppressed kinetic rifle, and a radar-absorbent shell, around 734 was no longer a life-saving insect but a predatory steel wolf.

Deployed by airdrop, 734 moved like a ghost through the canyons, its systems actively jamming enemy sensors and its profile all but invisible. It identified the target—a mobile electronic warfare hub—and from a ridge a mile away, its kinetic rifle spat a single, near-silent tungsten dart, shattering the truck's primary transmission dish. Before the enemy could even register the attack,734 vanished.

When the enemy fell back to a fortified cave complex, Unit 734 rendezvoused with other Axon cores at a supply connex near the drop off location to prepare for the follow-on direct assault. It built itself into a brutal bipedal form, a walking tank, attaching the thickest composite armor, a rotary cannon, and a missile pod.

The assault was a symphony of coordinated destruction. The Axon units advanced under a hail of fire. A high-explosive shell detonated against 734's right arm, obliterating the rotary cannon and shredding the appendage into slag and sparking wires. Half its offensive capability was gone in an instant. Its tactical subroutines screamed for it to fall back to a repair point, but its core AI, calculating probabilities in nanoseconds, overrode them. Instead, it identified a new resource.

Under the suppressing fire of its squadmates, 734 sprinted, its metal feet clanging on the rocky ground, not toward the rear, but toward the smoking wreck of an abandoned civilian construction vehicle. Its three core arms emerged, a blur of motion. In seconds, they cut through the rust-pitted steel of the vehicle's frame, tearing a heavy-duty hydraulic piston—once used to lift a backhoe's arm—free from its housing. With a screech of tortured metal, it ripped the massive component loose.

No time for perfect integration, it physically welded the base of the hydraulic ram directly onto the mangled stump of its right arm. It was a crude, ugly fusion of military hardware and scavenged industrial junk. There was no complex fire control; the AI simply programmed the arm to use the piston as a battering ram, a single-use, high-impact melee siege device. Less than forty seconds after being disarmed, 734 charged the nearest enemy bunker. It slammed its improvised arm forward, the hydraulic piston extending with catastrophic force, punching a huge, jagged hole through the reinforced concrete.

But its mission was not over. The enemy leadership had retreated into the deepest, most secure level of the bunker, accessible only through a narrow ventilation shaft. Unit 734 began its final transformation of the day. It built a long, serpentine body: a segmented chain of actuators and magnetic grips. It equipped itself with a plasma cutter and a single, high-yield explosive. The mechanical snake slithered into the darkness of the shaft to attach the charge. Shortly after reemerging, a muffled boom signaled the end of the enemy's command structure. The entire war was over a few weeks later.

A new order arrived: a naval drydock needed emergency repairs on the specialized radar-absorbent hull coating of a next-generation destroyer. The core scuttled to the racks, reaching for magnetic clamps, ultrasonic welders, and spidery limbs for clinging to the vast steel hull. The killer became a shipwright, its purpose shifting as easily as its form. It was not a soldier or a builder; it was a solution. A single, adaptable mind in a body of infinite possibility, ready to break or to build, whatever the mission required.

# 32

# AFTER MATH

Anders had always known his writing was strange. Flash fiction about talking animals wasn't exactly a booming market, but it was the only thing that ever felt like his voice. He arranged his collected works into what he believed was the perfect sequence, though half still lacked titles. Of the few pieces he'd published, even fewer had earned more than token payments. His biggest success was a 1,500-word fantasy called *Math,* which Clarkesworld bought for a little over two hundred dollars. The story's quirky premise — animals in the sprawling forest of "Arithmos" living by ancient principles known as "Math": Addition, Subtraction, Division, and Multiplication — earned him a sliver of notoriety among friends, and he shared its summary with anyone willing to listen.

But the story he believed in most — the one he quietly hoped might outlive him — was the one he still called *After Math,* stylizing it like the first century A.D. editor who assembled the treatise we know as Aristotle's Metaphysics. He'd researched and rewritten it obsessively, weaving emotion with a surprisingly accurate history of Military Working Dogs. Unlike his earlier attempts at giving antagonists meaningful lessons, this one let the underdog win — and offered a moral that wasn't just a counterpoint to the villain's, but something gentler, deeper.

He had written it during a time when he himself felt like an imposter, unsure whether his work mattered to anyone. Maybe that was why he'd poured so much of his own doubt — and his own hope — into the Labrador at the heart of the story.

* * *

"You're not a real service dog," Brutus scoffed. The Belgian Malinois, a decorated Military Working Dog, towered over Shadow, a young Labrador Retriever certified as an emotional support animal.

Shadow had been trying to help a nervous child in the waiting room only moments earlier, but

Brutus's voice cut through her confidence like a cold wind.

Dutch, a broad-chested German Shepherd from SWAT, added, "He's rude, but he's not wrong. At least other Labs get trained for narcotics, explosives, or search and rescue. Emotional support? That's barely service work."

Shadow's tail faltered. She knew she was a good girl — she *felt* it when people's breathing steadied under her touch — but their words made her feel small.

Brutus and Dutch were legends in the working-dog world, known for their skill and their disdain for what they called "Soft Service." They respected Seeing Eye Dogs, but emotional support animals ranked at the bottom of their hierarchy.

Shadow swallowed hard. "I help people," she said quietly. "Just… in a different way."

Dutch snorted, but something in his eyes flickered — not quite agreement, but not dismissal either.

Brutus launched into a sweeping monologue about the history of Military Working Dogs: their ancient origins, their evolution into highly trained partners, their unmatched senses, their heroism in war. Dutch settled into a commanding sit and ordered Shadow to do the same, his tone dismissive but his posture betraying a grudging respect for Brutus's storytelling.

Brutus spoke of early combat dogs, of the War Dog Program of 1942, of legendary canines like

Chips — the German Shepherd mix who attacked a machine-gun nest in Italy. Dutch rose, circled to ease his stiff joints, then resumed a stance that radiated authority. Shadow listened, awed and increasingly aware of how little she knew about her own role in the world.

But she also noticed something else: Brutus's voice softened when he spoke of the dogs who never came home. There was pride there, yes — but also grief.

As Brutus's speech wound down, a young man shuffled past them, shoulders slumped, eyes hollow.

Dutch sat immediately — his drug-detection training signaling a near-certain hit. Brutus tensed, ready for confrontation.

Shadow stepped forward before she could talk herself out of it.

She nudged the man's hand. He paused, then knelt, resting his forehead briefly against hers. A thin, aching smile crossed his face as a tear slipped down his cheek.

"Thanks, sweetie," he whispered. "I really needed that."

Shadow's tail wagged softly, pride blooming in her chest. Brutus and Dutch watched in silence. Joy and tenderness had been trained out of them long ago — but not forgotten.

Dutch exhaled, long and low. "Huh," he murmured. "Didn't think… well. Good work."

Brutus didn't speak, but his ears dipped — the smallest nod of respect.

Shadow stayed a moment longer, basking in the quiet certainty of her purpose.

* * *

Anders's alpha readers loved the concept but pointed out structural gaps and character inconsistencies. His beta readers — members of his target audience — helped him refine pacing and dialogue. One suggested renaming *After Math* to *Beyond Shadow's Doubt,* and Anders immediately knew it was right.

He realized, reading their notes, that he had written Shadow's journey to understand his own: that value isn't measured by the loudest accomplishments, but by the quiet moments when someone truly needs you.

With a few final tweaks, he felt satisfied. Now he only had thirty-nine untitled stories left — and the daunting task of figuring out how to publish them.

But for the first time in a long while, he didn't doubt himself.

Not beyond Shadow's doubt.

## 33

## GRANDPA'S BIRTHDAY

His was a blessed life, no doubt. Ed and his wife Sue-Ellen retired just outside of Tampa. The sun, a splendid, simmering sphere, spilled its golden grace over their cozy cottage, a quaint corner of the world painted in pastels. Palm fronds performed a perpetual, peaceful ballet in the balmy breeze. Everything was, for all intents and purposes, perfect. But a persistent, pestering pang of peculiar quietude often punctuated their paradise.

They had spent their salad days under the searing sun of Barstow, California, a dusty diamond in the rough desert. It was there they'd met, married, and meticulously molded a meaningful life. Their modest, middle-class home had been a boisterous, bubbling hub of happiness—home to three beautiful, bouncing boys: Ben, Bobby, and Bartholomew. The boys were their pride, their projects, their perpetual motion machines. From fixing battered bicycles to celebrating school successes, Ed and Sue-Ellen's world spun around their sons. The days had been a delightful delirious dance of duty and devotion.

Now, those days were distant dreams. Ben, a brilliant barrister, built his life in Boston, busy with briefs and his two bright, bookish boys. Bobby, a bold builder of bridges, was based in Boise, blessed with a lovely wife and a delightful daughter who was the apple of her granddad's eye. And Bartholomew, their baby, a marine biologist of magnificent merit, had made his home on the majestic shores of Maui with his wonderful wife and their four fantastic, fun-loving children. All their sons were successful, solid citizens who had started spectacular families of their own. Ed and Sue-Ellen couldn't be prouder, but pride was a poor proxy for presence. The quiet cottage in Tampa felt a thousand times larger than their bustling Barstow bungalow ever had.

To fill the creeping quiet, they found fellowship in service. Tuesdays were for the Tampa Bay Turtle Watch, where they walked the shores, searching for signs of nests, their silver hair shimmering in the sun. Sue-Ellen, with her soft smile and soothing sentences, spent her Thursdays reading stories to starry-eyed students at the local library. Ed, ever the handyman, hammered and honed away at the community center, fixing rickety chairs and wobbly windows, his work a welcome, wearing distraction.

Each morning, they made a ritual of walking the beach, the sand a soft, silken carpet under their seasoned feet. Ed had a peculiar pastime; he was on a permanent, patient pilgrimage to find the perfect seashell for Sue-Ellen. "Behold!" he'd declare, presenting a specimen with a flourish. "Is this not the paragon of pearlescence, the sovereign of spirals?"

Sue-Ellen would take the shell, turn it over in her delicate palm, and with a twinkle in her eye, playfully pronounce, "It's a very nice shell, dear. Perhaps the second-best shell on the beach today." Ed would feign a dramatic sigh, and they'd continue their walk, hand in hand, the hunt for the perfect shell a sweet, simple strand in the tapestry of their days.

Still, evenings were the hardest. After a dinner of simple, savory sustenance, they'd settle in the living room. Photographs, precious portals to the past, populated every surface. There were the boys, gap-toothed and grinning in Little League uniforms. There were weddings, graduations, and the first fuzzy photos of their grandchildren. The faces smiled back, frozen in joyous frames, a beautiful but bittersweet reminder of the boisterous life they once led. Video calls with Boston and Boise were bright spots, but the ten-hour time difference to Hawaii made connecting with Bartholomew's bunch a complicated calculation. The loneliness would creep in then, a cool, quiet tide washing over the warmth of their love.

"It's silly, isn't it?" Sue-Ellen murmured one evening, tracing the face of her youngest grandson in a photo. "To have so much, to be so blessed, and still feel... a little bit bare."

Ed wrapped his arm around her. "It's not silly, Sue-Ellen. It's love. We're just so full of it, it has to go somewhere."

The week of Ed's seventy-first birthday dawned dazzling and bright. The air was alive with the scent of salt and sweet plumeria drifting on the breeze. Sue-Ellen had planned a simple, splendid day: a morning walk, a fine fish dinner at their favorite seaside spot, and a special strawberry shortcake, Ed's favorite.

They began their birthday beachcombing, the sun just beginning its spectacular ascent. The waves whispered sweet secrets to the shore. Ed, in his usual fashion, was scanning the sand for his elusive prize. He stooped, spotting a sand dollar of significant size. "Sue-Ellen, my sweet! Surely, this is it! The supreme sand dollar! The-"

He stopped mid-sentence. His eyes, and then Sue-Ellen's, were drawn to a peculiar point on the placid, purple-blue plane of the morning sea. A shape was moving toward them, steady and serene. It was too large to be a drifting log, too low to be a boat. As it drew nearer, its form became fantastically, unbelievably clear.

It was a colossal sea turtle, ancient and awesome, its powerful flippers paddling with a placid, purposeful rhythm. And on its broad, barnacle-studded back, it towed a tidy, trim little raft. On the raft, waving with wild, wonderful glee, were four small figures, their silhouettes sharp against the shimmering sea.

Ed's jaw dropped. Sue-Ellen's hands flew to her mouth, her gasp lost in the gentle roar of the surf. It was impossible. It was incredible. It was Bartholomew's bunch. It was Iokeline, Akelaika, Mikiala, and Elenola.

The grand turtle, with a final, graceful glide, guided the raft right to the shore, nudging it gently onto the wet sand. Four small pairs of feet hit the ground running.

"Grandpa! Grandma!"

The quiet of the Tampa coast was gloriously, gratifyingly shattered by the gleeful greetings of their grandchildren. Four small bodies slammed into them, a tidal wave of hugs and happiness. Ed found himself lifting little Elenola high in the air, her laughter a melody more magical than any birdsong. Sue-Ellen was enveloped by Akelaika and Mikiala, while Ilokeline, the eldest, beamed, her smile as bright as the burgeoning day.

"Happy Birthday, Grandpa!" they chorused, a cacophony of cheer.

Bartholomew and his wife appeared as if from a

dream, walking from a little way down the beach where they'd been waiting. The logistics, Bartholomew later explained with a laugh, involved a very early flight into Tampa International, a pre-arranged and perplexing pact with a particularly perceptive sea turtle (a long story involving a rescued fishing net and a shared love of sea grass), and a whole lot of hope.

The day was a whirlwind of wonder. Their quiet cottage was transformed into a castle of joyous chaos. The air filled with the sounds Ed and Sue-Ellen had missed so dearly: the pitter-patter of running feet, the shrieks of playful discovery, and the incessant, inquisitive "why?" that is the hallmark of a happy child. They built a fantastic fortress of furniture, read stories in silly voices until they were hoarse, and baked the strawberry shortcake with a chaotic committee of small, flour-dusted chefs.

For dinner, they didn't go out. They had a picnic on the living room floor—a fantastic feast of fish sticks and French fries, a meal more magnificent than any five-star fare. Ed, seated in the center of it all, felt a profound, perfect peace settle over him. The pang of loneliness was gone, replaced by an overwhelming, overflowing love. He caught Sue-Ellen's eye across the happy havoc, and she gave him a watery, wonderful smile that said everything.

As the afternoon sun began its slow, spectacular slide into the sea, painting the sky in strokes of orange, pink, and purple, it was time for the magical journey home. The great sea turtle had been waiting patiently in the shallows, munching on sea lettuce.

There were long hugs and promises of another visit soon. "Thank you for the best birthday ever, my little wonders," Ed said, his voice thick with emotion.

"We love you, Grandpa! We love you, Grandma!" they called, clambering back onto the raft.

With a final wave, the children were off. The ancient turtle began its powerful, placid paddle, pulling the raft away from the shore and into the heart of the fiery sunset. Ed and Sue-Ellen stood on the beach, arm in arm, watching until the little raft was just a speck against the vast, vibrant canvas of the sky. The house would be quiet again, but it was a different kind of quiet now. It was a peaceful quiet, filled with the echoes of laughter, the warmth of recent hugs, and the sweet, sticky memory of strawberry shortcake.

As the last sliver of the sun sank below the horizon, Ed's foot nudged something in the sand. He bent down and picked it up. It was a conch shell, flawlessly formed, its spiral a perfect poem of the sea. Its lip was lined with a shimmering, pearlescent pink that seemed to hold all the colors of the sunset they had just witnessed.

He held it out to his wife. "Sue-Ellen," he said softly.

She took it, her fingers tracing its exquisite form. She looked from the shell, to her husband's loving face, and back out to the empty, beautiful sea.

"Ed," she whispered, a tear of pure joy tracing a path down her cheek. "It's perfect."

# BONUS STORY

All of the previous stories were in the Flash Fiction category, which means they were not more than 1,500 words in length. The bonus story, however, is set apart because it is considerably longer, yet I wanted to include it with this collection. I hope you have enjoyed the stories and that you'll like this one, as well.

# THE FLAME MAGE AND THE SAVER OF KNOWLEDGE

The world, on the morning it began to end, was behaving with perfect ordinariness. Bakers pulled golden loaves from ovens that breathed warmth into cobblestone streets. Bankers counted coins behind brass-barred windows, their ledgers aligned in tidy columns. Schoolchildren traced letters on slate boards while their teachers drew the curtains against the spring glare. It was the kind of morning that made you believe tomorrow would arrive looking very much like today.

It was, of course, exactly the kind of morning that precedes disaster.

The first sign was a column of fire so intense it turned the midday sky the color of a bruised peach. It erupted from the heart of the Grand Municipal Library — that ancient institution whose marble steps had been worn smooth by a thousand years of curious feet. The pillar climbed higher than the cathedral spires, and the sound it made was not the roar you might expect but a sustained, mournful exhalation, as though the building itself were sighing its last breath.

Brave souls rushed in. Librarians clutching armfuls of manuscripts. A janitor named Giles who went back three times for the children's wing and did not come out a fourth. A visiting scholar from the eastern provinces who shielded a crate of irreplaceable star charts with her own body and was found afterward, singed but alive, still holding them against her chest. The star charts survived. Giles did not. Neither did four hundred thousand volumes of accumulated human thought — philosophy, poetry, agricultural science, fairy tales, tax law, or the love letters bound in ribbon and donated by a sentimental widow in the year of the great flood.

Anchors in pressed suits struggled to maintain composure. "An act of unprecedented cultural terrorism," they called it, and for once the gravity of the language was not exaggeration. The perpetrator's name was el Rey del Fuego. The Flame Mage. A figure wreathed in shimmering heat who had declared war — not on armies, not on governments, but on knowledge itself.

His philosophy was elemental in its cruelty: erase the past, and you control the future. Burn what people know, and they will accept what you tell them.

The scene repeated itself – in port cities, mountain towns, villages so small they had only a single shelf of shared books in the post office. Always the same pillar of flame, always that terrible sigh. Norman Pfefferkorn, a pretzel seller on the corner of Maple and Broad, was extolling his artisanal salt crystals to a disinterested passerby when the reading room across the street exploded in a cascade of amber light. Norman screamed, flung his tray of salted twists into the air like a startled bird releasing its feathers, ran three full blocks before realizing he was heading toward the fire, reversed course, tripped over a hydrant, and sat on the curb weeping into a crushed pretzel.

It would have been funny if everything weren't so terribly sad.

* * *

Elena had ink-stained fingers. She'd had them since the age of seven, when she first discovered that a pen was not merely a writing instrument but a key that opened every door the world kept stubbornly locked. She had a mind like a meticulously ordered index: cross-referenced, annotated, and filed under headings both practical and whimsical. She could tell you the melting point of copper and the name of the fairy queen in the fourth tale of the Greenwood Cycle.

The libraries had been her home. Not in the metaphorical sense people use when they say a coffee shop is "like home" — she meant it with the full weight of the word. The library was the place where Elena felt the floor solid beneath her, where the air tasted right, where the world's bewildering chaos resolved into navigable order.

Growing up, she had always found people confusing. Social interactions operated by rules no one would write down — expectations that shifted with context and facial expressions she couldn't always read. But in books, characters' motivations were explained, chaos had structure and conflict resolved. Even tragedy made sense on the page in ways it never did in the hallway outside her classroom, where laughter could mean joy or cruelty and she was never sure which.

Her parents were both academics, her mother an historian of maritime trade routes and her father a linguist specializing in dead languages. They encouraged her to read with the same benign enthusiasm with which they encouraged her to eat vegetables. They were kind, distracted people who perhaps mistook their daughter's quietness for contentment. Either they missed her underlying loneliness, or they simply didn't know what to do about it, being rather lonely people themselves.

When her town's library burned, Elena stood in the street and watched embers drift upward like dying fireflies. Something inside her cracked, but it did not crumble. It reforged. She knelt in the ash and picked up a half-burned page. One side was destroyed; the other still bore a passage from a botanical encyclopedia, describing the pollination habits of evening primrose. She read it twice, folded it carefully, and placed it in her coat pocket.

She would become the Saver of Knowledge.

The plan materialized with the same ruthless precision she applied to everything. On the edge of town, perched on a spit of rock above the grey sea, stood an abandoned lighthouse scheduled for demolition — though the paperwork had "conveniently vanished" in a small fire at the records office, a coincidence Elena found darkly appropriate, given the circumstances.

She established a strict routine. By night, she hauled supplies: reams of paper liberated from an office supply warehouse whose owner had fled south; bottles of ink procured through means she preferred not to examine too closely; pens, pencils, a battered typewriter missing its Q key. By day, she wrote— alphabets, multiplication tables, thermodynamics, history reconstructed from memory and cross-checked against charred fragments scavenged from ruins.

The work was maddening. Her memory, formidable as it was, had gaps — infuriating lacunae where critical facts should have been. She would sit for hours trying to recall whether the Treaty of Silver Falls was signed in the third or fourth year of Queen

Margarethe's reign, berating herself: *You should know this. A real bibliognost would know this.* Then she would shake her head, pick up the pen, and write what she remembered, leaving margins for corrections that may never come.

The lighthouse filled with the rustle of paper and the scent of fresh ink, a perfume she found more comforting than lavender. Rumors circulated about spies sniffing around for intellectual activity like bloodhounds in pursuit. Elena drew the curtains tighter and worked by candlelight. She previously dreamed of being an author, writing novels that would rest on the shelves, spines cracked from rereading. That dream had become a luxury. This mission was a necessity.

* * *

Elliot found the lighthouse quite by accident. He was sixteen, with unruly black hair and quick, curious eyes the color of river stones. He'd come hunting spare parts for a self-buttering toaster — a device that, so far, had succeeded only in launching pats of butter at the ceiling with alarming velocity. He hadn't expected to find the door ajar and the interior transformed into something that made his breath catch.

Stacks of paper rose from floor to ceiling, organized into columns and rows that followed a system only their creator could fully parse. Handwritten pages hung from clotheslines, drying like laundry. A typewriter clattered above. The air smelled of ink and sea salt and purpose.

"It's . . ." Elliot breathed, turning in a slow circle. "It's a *library*."

Elena appeared at the top of the spiral staircase like a sentinel, her face rigid with sharp, immediate fear. "No one can know," she said. Her voice was low and urgent, stripped of pleasantry.

He looked at her — ink on her fingers, exhaustion bruising the skin beneath her eyes, a pen tucked behind each ear — and understood immediately. Not just what she was doing, but why it mattered. "I won't tell," he said. Then, after a pause: "Can I help?"

And so the lighthouse gained its second keeper. Elena was the architect and curator — the mind that decided what must be preserved and in what order. Elliot became the engineer, building a hand-cranked printing press from bicycle parts and a repurposed waffle iron. It was loud, temperamental, and smelled faintly of breakfast, but it worked. Then, using enchanted crystals from an abandoned mineralogist's shop — stones impervious to fire, water, and time — he devised a method of encoding entire encyclopedias into a crystal the size of a walnut. Elena held the first completed stone up to the lamplight, watched its facets glimmer with compressed knowledge, and for the first time in months, she smiled.

Together, they were a two-person revolution.

It was Elliot who made the discovery that changed everything. While searching through the debris of a smaller branch library — a modest building that had served a farming community and still smelled of smoke and heartbreak — he found a hidden metal box bolted beneath a collapsed desk. Inside, singed but intact, lay a librarian's journal. Most entries were mundane: supply orders, patron complaints, a terse note about someone returning a book with jam on page forty-seven. But one entry, dated months before the burnings began, stopped Elliot cold.

**June 4th** — A strange incident today. A young man from the countryside, Fernando I believe he called himself, presented a manuscript to Head Librarian Hemlock. It was an odd little book, yet it seemed to buzz with peculiar energy. The boy was so earnest, his eyes shining with hope. Hemlock, in his usual imperious fashion, didn't grant the work a cursory glance and dismissed the boy with a wave. I saw the light in the young man's eyes die. It was a cruel, needless act. I intended to retrieve the manuscript from the bin later, but it was gone. I fear Hemlock's pride may have planted a dangerous seed today. There was a power in that boy — a fire I did not like.

* * *

Elliot brought the journal to Elena. They sat together on the lighthouse steps as the sun bled into the sea, reading the entry twice, three times. Neither spoke for a long while.

"Fernando," Elena said quietly, testing the name. It was a human name. An ordinary name. The name of a boy who had once walked to a library with aspirations gleaming in his eyes.

"He wasn't always the Flame Mage," Elliot said.

"No," Elena replied. "He wasn't."

A flicker of something complicated passed between them. Understanding was a country with difficult borders, and they had just glimpsed its coastline.

* * *

Their work was discovered through a combination of bad luck and human carelessness. A fisherman spotted candlelight in the lighthouse and mentioned it to a tavern keeper who told a merchant who told a stranger in a long coat who listened with great interest and tipped generously.

Three days later, a cloaked figure was spotted at the edge of the village, standing motionless on the hill road, staring toward the sea. The next night, an intense glow bloomed on the horizon – not the gentle amber of sunset but a fierce, pulsing vermillion that set the clouds alight.

Elena saw it from the lighthouse window and went very still. The pen slipped from her fingers and rolled across the desk, coming to rest against a stack of freshly inked pages on ornithological migration patterns. She did not pick it up.

"He's coming," she said.

El Rey del Fuego walked toward them across the headland, and the grass withered in his wake. He was taller than Elena had imagined — gaunt, sharp-featured, wrapped in a mantle of living flame that rippled and crackled with each step. His laughter preceded him, a sound like cascading popping embers, bright and brittle yet devoid of warmth.

Norman Pfefferkorn, who had — by staggering coincidence — come to the coastal village to "get away from it all" was enjoying a quiet evening with a bag of his own pretzels on a bench overlooking the harbor. When the inferno neared, he leapt to his feet and ran in three frantic circles, shouting something that might have been "Fire!" or might have been "Pretzels!" — witnesses later disagreed — before tripping over the same bench he'd been sitting on and sprawling face-first into a hydrangea bush. He remained there, whimpering softly, for the duration of the confrontation.

Elena climbed the spiral staircase to the top of the lighthouse. Elliot scrambled up behind her, his satchel of tools clanking against the iron railing.

"Saver of Knowledge," the Flame Mage called, his voice carrying the dry rasp of a forest fire consuming ancient timber. "Come down."

Elena gripped the railing, knuckles white. Her heart hammered as though trying to escape without her. But she had spent a lifetime learning to function with fear, apprehensive of speaking in class, being noticed, or being found wanting. Fear was an old companion she knew well.

She leaned over the railing. "Why are you doing this? Why do you hate knowledge?"

The Flame Mage's fiery aura dimmed. Not extinguished — diminished, as though a hand had turned down a lamp. When he spoke again, his voice had changed. The theatrical menace was gone, replaced by something rawer, something laced with cold, ancient pain.

"Hate it?" He laughed — a short, broken sound. "I *loved* it. I loved it more than anything in this wretched world. I walked two hundred miles to stand in the shadow of the Grand Library. Two hundred miles, in shoes that fell apart on the road, eating nothing but hard bread and creek water, because I believed — I truly believed — that knowledge was the great equalizer. That if you had something worth saying, someone would listen."

His flames flickered lower. In the guttering light, Elena could almost see the boy he had been — dusty, travel-worn, trembling with anticipation.

"I held my life's work in my hands. A treatise on using elemental magic to bring prosperity to rural communities — irrigation powered by thermal currents, heating for homes that couldn't afford fuel, light for villages that had never seen a streetlamp. I had bound it in leather I saved a year to buy. Everything I knew, everything I dreamed, was in that manuscript."

His voice dropped to a whisper that somehow carried farther than his shouts.

"I gave it to the Head Librarian. He didn't open it. He held it in one hand, weighed it like a fishmonger weighing a catch, and looked at my dusty clothes, calloused hands, and country accent. And he smiled — a smile as cold as winter stone — and said, 'Amateurs have no place here.'"

The fire around him surged briefly, a spasm of remembered humiliation.

"The scholars behind him laughed. Sniggering into their sleeves like children mocking a beggar. And I left. I walked back down those marble steps, manuscript in hand, found a quiet alley, and burned it. I burned my own work — my own *heart* — because they made me ashamed of it."

He raised his eyes to Elena, and they were molten.

"That humiliation didn't fade. It *grew*. And I discovered I had power. Raw fire magic — the kind that doesn't need a library card or a scholar's approval. Fire is simple. Pure. Absolute. It doesn't discriminate. It treats a king's palace and a peasant's shack with perfect equality."

He pointed a burning finger at the lighthouse.

"And you — you hide in your tower, hoarding your precious words just like they did! You think these highfalutin works make you better than everyone else? That your alphabets and taxonomies are anything but walls? Weapons the 'knowledgeable' use to keep everyone else out?" I am *freeing* everyone from your tyranny! When there is only one truth — *my* truth — everyone will finally be equal!"

He hurled a blazing sphere at the lighthouse. It struck the stone wall below Elena and exploded in a shower of sparks. The tower shuddered. Pages — hundreds of handwritten pages — caught fire and whirled upward like burning birds.

Elena stared at the falling ash of her work and felt the grief strike her like a physical blow. Months of labor. Irreplaceable reconstructions. Gone.

But Elliot seized her arm. "Up here! I have an idea!" He was already pulling something from his satchel — a crystal, larger than the ones they'd used for storage, cut with dozens of precise facets. He'd been working on it in secret for weeks: a new lens for the old lamp housing.

"It's not just a storage device," he said, hands shaking as he fitted it into the lamp's aperture. "It's a projector. Elena — we can't hide the materials. We have to *share* them."

The aperture on Elena's understanding opened wide. She had been so focused on *saving* books, hoarding information behind locked doors, that she had forgotten the very thing books had taught her. Knowledge isn't meant to be locked in a tower. It's meant to be shared, given freely, pressed into the hands of anyone who reaches for it. Its true power lies not in preservation but in proliferation. She had been protecting knowledge the way a miser protects gold — and in doing so, she had, without realizing it, echoed the very gatekeeping that had created Fernando.

Below, the Flame Mage gathered his power for another assault. The air around him thickened with heat, and the grassy patches of sand beneath his feet turned to emerald-streaked glass.

Elliot aimed the crystal lens at the sky and nodded to Elena. "Tell them a story."

Elena opened her mouth, and her voice — amplified by the crystal's magic until it boomed across the land, clear as a cathedral bell — rang out into the night.

She did not recite dry facts. She did not list dates or theorems. She wove a tale — a story about a brave baker who hid books in bread loaves, a clever banker who encoded poems in financial reports, heroes who dared to think for themselves when thinking was forbidden. The beam of light burst from the lighthouse lamp, and within it, shimmering words and images unfurled across the night sky — a tale written in light, projected across the clouds, illuminated in radiant colors by the very force meant to destroy them.

Across the village, across the countryside, across the sleeping towns and darkened cities, people looked up. They saw the story blazing in the sky and remembered — tales their grandparents had told, ideas they had once debated freely, songs they had forgotten they knew. A baker in a flour-dusted apron stepped out of his shop and wept. A banker set down her ledger and whispered the opening line of a poem she'd loved as a child.

El Rey del Fuego faltered. His flames shrank. He hurled fire at the images in the sky — great roaring torrents of it — and they passed right through. The words shimmered, reformed, continued.

He screamed and threw more fire, but he could not burn the light. He could not burn an idea.

Elliot adjusted the crystal's frequency with a small clockwork dial. A harmonic resonance — tuned to the wavelength of elemental fire magic — pulsed outward. The flames surrounding el Rey del Fuego flickered, sputtered, coughed like a candle in a draft. His mantle of fire unraveled in streamers of dying light, peeling away like burning paper in reverse. Beneath it, just for a moment, Elena saw a young man — dusty, thin, with eyes that had once shone with hope.

With a final, defiant shriek — a sound of fury and grief and something that might, in a gentler world, have been called heartbreak — he was extinguished. Where el Rey del Fuego had stood was a pile of warm silt, slowly cooling in the sea breeze, and the lingering smell of burnt sugar.

* * *

In the aftermath, there was celebration — cautious at first, then joyful, then raucous. Bonfires were lit, which caused a brief collective flinch before everyone remembered that not all fire was bad.

Someone found Norman Pfefferkorn still lodged in the hydrangea bush, and after he was extracted with care and given a blanket and a cup of tea, he immediately began describing the evening's events in a version that bore only a passing resemblance to reality.

The leaders and officials came wearing ceremonial sashes, smelling of cologne and cautious optimism. They offered Elena the position of Royal Librarian and a corresponding palace — marble floors, a staff of forty, an unlimited acquisition budget, her name carved above the entrance.

Elena hesitated.

She stood at the top of the damaged lighthouse while Elliot was below already sketching plans for a network of community-run light-libraries. The sea wind carried the salt-and-ash smell of the night's battle. Below her, the cheering crowds were a warm, distant hum.

The adrenaline was fading, and in its absence, a subtle calm washed over her like a landscape after the rain: everything rinsed clean, and every color brighter. She looked inward and found something new there: a quiet, steady confidence, born not from certainty but from the act of standing firm when everything in her had wanted to hide.

She thought about Fernando. About a boy who had loved knowledge and been turned away. About how the gates of learning could become walls if the people inside forgot to open them. She thought about herself — the shy girl who had hidden in books because people were too unpredictable, who had built a lighthouse full of words and locked the door. Her whole life, she had been the only person in a room full of records — safe, surrounded, and alone.

Now she understood. Sharing knowledge meant sharing *herself* — stepping out of the sanctuary of solitude, risking the mess and confusion of other people, accepting that the world outside the page would never be as orderly as the world within it. It was terrifying. It was necessary. It was, she realized with a small, surprised laugh, what she had wanted all along.

She descended the stairs and faced the officials.

"I'm honored," she said, and meant it. "But no. The compiled experiences of all don't belong to one person or in one place." She gestured toward Elliot's sketches, toward the crystal still glowing softly in the lamp housing, toward the sky where, if you looked carefully, you could still see the faintest ghost of the story she'd told, lingering among the stars like a benediction. "Knowledge should be like light — everywhere at once, belonging to all and impossible to cage."

She and Elliot took their plans and their crystals and traveled the world. They taught communities to build their own libraries —warm, welcoming places where a farmer's almanac sat beside a philosopher's treatise and both were valued equally. They taught people to write their own stories and project them into the night sky, so that every village had its own constellation of tales, its own galaxy of shared understanding.

Elena was no longer simply the Saver of Knowledge. She had become its greatest champion — ensuring that no single flame could ever again create an all-consuming darkness, because you cannot burn what lives in a thousand minds and shines from a thousand towers.

And the world carried on, as the world does. Bakers baked. Bankers banked. Schoolchildren traced their letters on slate boards — and now, on clear nights, they looked up from their work and saw stories blazing among the stars, written in light above their rooftops.

Norman Pfefferkorn, it should be noted, recounted versions more elaborate with each telling. By the end, he had personally wrestled the Flame Mage into submission using nothing but a bag of pretzels and his "signature move." Nobody believed him, but everyone listened, and he always sold a great many pretzels afterward.

Which, when you think about it, is exactly what a good story is supposed to do.

*— THE END —*

# ABOUT THE AUTHOR

Jeff William Linzey is a Brazilian Jiu Jitsu Black Belt, board-game strategist, and award-winning guacamole craftsman who was once voted by his law school class as "the one I'd least want to oppose at trial."

Aside from his JD, his ties to learned professions further extend to being a licensed minister, and beyond a tendency to research and self-diagnose ailments, he married an ER nurse.

His professional writing has been recognized as one of the ten best of its semicentennial and republished in the 50th Anniversary Edition, but this collection marks his first published work of fiction—unless you count the children's story he co-wrote with his four imaginative kids.

Jeff lives with his wonderful wife Nicole, their four fantastic children—Jocelyn, Adelaide, Michaela, and Eleanor—and an ever-growing stack of books he swears he'll finish soon.

www.ingramcontent.com/pod-product-compliance
Lightning Source LLC
La Vergne TN
LVHW090517110826
845146LV00003B/896

* 9 7 9 8 9 9 6 0 8 2 7 0 4 *